MW00881775

WHERE DARKNESS CASTS A SHADOW
By Linda Alcorn

Remember... beyond every shadow there is sunlight.

Linda

To my best friend Anita,
who also happens to be my real-life sister.
Thank you for your love, support, encouragement, and
dog-sitting. We would <u>all</u> truly be lost without you.
I love you with all my heart.

Nothing is what it seems in a place where darkness casts a shadow. No one can be trusted. Nobody is safe.

Chapter One

Darkness sprawled across the sky as the sun sank slowly behind the jagged hillside. A lone bird dashed in and out of the daylight, heading eastward toward Vera Keller's home. Vera sat quietly at her bedroom window and studied the bird's curious behavior. He was moving at an unbelievable rate of speed and with seemingly malevolent intentions. Curiosity turned to fear as the bird's silhouette grew wider and wider. He was not small. He was not a bird. Vera was suddenly face to face with a dragon. A puff of smoke billowed from his nostrils. The 76-year-old grandmother spun around to shield herself just as a firestorm erupted from the dragon's angry jowls. The room was fully engulfed, but amidst the smoke and flames Vera spotted something in the hallway beyond her bedroom door – a woman's body crumpled lifelessly on the floor in a pool of blood. The terror roused her violently from her slumber.

Vera opened her eyes to total darkness just as she had done every morning for the last two years. Nine days before her 75th birthday, a massive stroke blinded Vera in both eyes and damaged her heart irreparably. Dreaming restored her eyesight temporarily each night, but as her health deteriorated, the dreams became more frightening. She became convinced that her recurring nightmares, like this one, were actually clairvoyant visions warning of danger for her granddaughters. This vision scared the hell out of her. Fearing that her granddaughter London was the victim in this horrible nightmare, she quickly retrieved her call bell from her bedside table to summons London from down the hall. Her hands trembled as she listened for signs of life from London or her beloved dachshund named Vienna. She nervously rang the bell a second time just as the creaky hinges on her bedroom door announced London's arrival.

"Everything's okay. I'm here."

"Oh, London. I thought you were dead."

"I think you had another bad dream," London replied sensitively. She began helping her from beneath the blankets. "Do you need me to help you use the bathroom?"

Vera's voice wavered. "No. No. Go back to bed until morning."

"It is morning. It's time to get up, Grammy."

"But the girl..." Vera sputtered. "She was you. Tall and thin."

"I'm fine, Grammy. It was just another bad dream."

"She had flowing raven-black hair."

"Well, there you see. My hair is blonde now. Remember? I told you I changed the color. That girl wasn't me, Grammy."

"But I..."

London stroked her grandmother's hair as she peeled back the blanket and sheet covering her frail, trembling body. She lifted Vera's hand onto her shoulder and helped the old woman rise to a seated position. "We should get you out of bed now. Nurse Wendy will be here in 20 minutes."

"Where's Geneva? Is Geneva here yet?" Vera asked.

"No. She won't be here until tonight. Remember?" London sighed and kissed Vera's cheek.

Geneva was London's half sister who was given up for adoption as a baby. Vera's daughter, Sicily, was killed in a car accident. Geneva's father, Shawn, also died in that accident. The true identity of London's father became an unsolved mystery. Vera was forced to make a heart-wrenching decision. She agreed to raise London, who was five at the time, but could not care for an eight-month-old baby. Geneva was adopted by the Charles family from Louisiana and presumably lost forever. Then 27 years later, Geneva contacted Vera unexpectedly. The call came on April 11th, Vera's birthday. By June, plans were in place for her to spend the summer at Vera's home in Coral Leaf, West Virginia.

London was too young to remember her baby sister, but she worried the stressful reunion might shorten the limited time she had left with her grandmother. Nevertheless, her objections were overruled. Vera knew her heart was weakening; she struggled for breath most days by this point – even with help from her oxygen concentrator machine. Her dying wish was to hold her long-lost granddaughter in her arms just one more time.

"Let's get you into your chair so you can feel the sunshine over by the window," London continued. "I will fix you an English muffin with apricot jam. Then when Vienna finishes her breakfast she can come sit on your lap."

"Yes. Okay," Vera replied. She cooperated and said nothing more about the nightmare, but the images of that young woman continued haunting Vera throughout the day. She feared the worst for London and Geneva. She knew only one thing for certain... one of her granddaughters was in danger. Maybe both.

Geneva arrived at eight o'clock that evening. Vera was waiting impatiently in her wheelchair in the front foyer. London opened the door, smiled pleasantly, and invited her inside. Vera greeted her excitedly with a warm embrace and Geneva seemed equally excited about the reunion. Vera was thrilled. For London the scene was unsettling; Geneva's tears and exuberance seemed unnaturally sentimental given the situation. She was not the only one displeased by the stranger's arrival either. Vienna charged into the room moments later, growling and barking incessantly. London quieted the dog by removing her to the kitchen, but Vienna's reaction further substantiated her own misgivings. That dog's instincts were never wrong.

By the time London returned minutes later, Geneva had already pushed Vera and her wheelchair into the living room and was helping her move to the sofa.

"I'm so glad to have both of my girls here with me," Vera said.

"I am so happy to have a grandmother," Geneva said, taking a seat on the sofa beside her.

Vera stroked her long, silky-soft hair then gently traced her hands along the lines of her face. She was desperate for confirmation about the identity of the girl from her nightmare. "I bet you have beautiful, dark-colored hair. Don't you?"

"Yea, it's pretty dark. Why?"

"I think you were in my dream last night."

Geneva responded eagerly. "Really? What was the dream about?"

"I don't know yet." Vera folded her hands in her lap.

London glanced at Geneva. She was visibly confused, but didn't ask any further questions on the subject. Instead she just blurted out London's name.

"What?"

"Oh," Geneva chuckled. "I just said your name because it's so pretty."

"Thanks I guess. But I didn't pick it." She was not impressed by her half-sister's attempt at flattery.

"All your mother's idea," Vera said. "She wanted your names to inspire dreams beyond the boundaries of this sleepy, secluded town. When she was a little girl she insisted her name Sicily meant she was going to be a famous artist when she grew up." Vera sighed. Her eyes became teary. "She never made it to Italy like she dreamed, but she was happy. She loved to paint, but she loved you girls even more." Vera reached out in search of London's hand and urged her to join them on the sofa.

"Sounds like you miss her," Geneva said.

"Every day."

"She did the painting above the fireplace. With the mountains and the sunset," London added.

"She called it The View from my Bedroom Window. She was so creative," Vera said. "See how the mountain casts a heart-shaped reflection in the lake? Sicily called that spot Le Coeur du Lac."

Vera paused again and wiped a tear from her cheek.

"Is that French or something?" Geneva asked.

London swallowed hard to hold back some tears of her own. "The heart of the lake," she said.

Vera's hand trembled as she wrapped her fingers around the gold cross on her necklace. "I used to stare at the painting all the time. Especially after she died. It helped me feel close to her. I can't see it anymore, but I still picture it in my mind."

"Are you completely blind? Or is everything just really blurry?" Geneva asked.

London started to explain. "The stroke affected the posterior cerebral artery…"

"What does that mean?" Geneva interrupted.

Vera chuckled and shook her head. "It just means that my eye sight is gone."

"The doctor says that's also why her hands shake all the time and why she has such a hard time getting around," London explained.

Geneva moved closer to Vera on the sofa and clasped her hands in hers. "What else did the doctor say?"

"I don't listen to that silly doctor any more. It's all in God's hands now and when He decides it's time for me to go. My heart is starting to fail me now."

"Grammy, please don't talk like that," London said. "It's not your time yet."

"Oh, I'm not going anywhere just yet," Vera responded. "I have a feeling there's still work for me to do here."

"We ain't letting you go yet," Geneva said.

"We should probably get you to bed now though," London said. "You and Geneva will have the whole day together tomorrow while I'm at work."

Vera wanted to argue, but she understood that London's strict rules about bedtime were for her own good. "Perhaps Geneva could read to me for a little while before I go to sleep."

"Oh, I don't read very good. Especially out loud," Geneva said. "Anyways, I kinda' got plans. You don't mind do you, Grammy?"

"Not at all, dear."

"But you just got here," London objected, responding not only to Geneva's insensitivity, but also to her referring to their grandmother as Grammy. That was her special name for Vera. It was derived from the dual role she had played in London's life – grandmother and mommy. Geneva's casual use of the title was both presumptuous and insulting.

"I know, but the girl at the filling station said I should come to the bar where her brother works. Lots of people hang out there."

London shook her head judgmentally. "I guess I'll read to you tonight."

"I hope you're not too disappointed," Geneva said, leaning in close to kiss Vera on the cheek. "I promise I'll make it up to you. I just want to try and make some friends if I'm gonna' be here all summer."

"I'm not at all disappointed. You should go. Have fun," Vera replied.

Geneva offered to help Vera to bed, but London refused. Despite her harsh judgment for Geneva's decision to party instead of getting to know her grandmother, she was thankful for her departure. She wasn't willing to risk letting some uneducated, insensitive phony ruin the precious time she had left with her Grammy. She had managed just fine for the past two years with Nurse Wendy's help during the day; she didn't want or need anyone else's help. She did, however, need to vent her frustration. Her best friend, Brenna Reese, was her usual sounding board. Thankfully, they were scheduled to work together that next morning.

Before Vera's stroke, London worked 50 to 60 hours a week as an underwriter for Blue Ridge Mutual Insurance Company. The job paid well and afforded her a nice car and a cozy townhouse, but when Grammy got sick, London willingly cancelled her lease and moved back in. At the same time, she traded her promising career in the insurance industry for a part-time waitressing job at The Roger Street Diner. The work was mind-numbing and more physically demanding, but London had the scheduling flexibility she needed. The owners, Reverend Calvin Walker and his wife Collette, were long time friends of the Keller family. Before retiring, Calvin preached at the church where Vera taught Sunday school. London's Grampy, Montgomery Keller, attended church services regularly there too and even helped rebuild the steeple after it was struck by lightning.

The diner was located along the State Highway A corridor, which divided Coral Leaf from the neighboring town of Connors Bluff. The locale and hometown menu made the small restaurant popular with truck drivers and construction workers. That kept London and Brenna hustling during the early morning breakfast shift. By the time the crowd dispersed at seven-thirty, London was desperate for her fifteen minute break with Brenna. Brenna smoked. London ranted about her unwelcomed guest.

"I feel like my worst nightmare has come true," London said.

"Is she really that bad?"

"She's worse. She strolls in at eight o'clock last night, spends like twenty minutes with Grammy, and is out the door. She said she wanted to party. Can you believe that?"

"I thought the whole point was to get to know the family," Brenna said. "Isn't that what she told you?"

"That's what Grammy told me. I never actually talked to her; she always called while I was here."

"Maybe she just felt awkward. I mean she went her whole life without knowing her real family. That's gotta' make her head spin a little bit. Don't you think?"

London smiled and chuckled a little bit. "Maybe she sensed I hated her."

"You don't really hate her," Brenna replied. Her facial expression indicated both amusement and disapproval.

"I think I might."

"Come on, you don't hate anybody. Not even Brody."

London cringed and shook her head. "You swore to never mention that name again."

Brody Danbrook was a former boyfriend. He had charmed his way into London's heart, her bed, and her wallet. By the time she realized his motives, he had manipulated her into spending half her life savings. She later learned that his real interest was in the millions she stood to inherit from her grandmother's estate. She hadn't been in a relationship for a year and a half. She hadn't been on a date or had sex for almost three months, not since her top secret, for-old-times-sake fling with her high school boyfriend, Burt Anderson.

"It's not your fault, London. I fell for the guy's sweet talking too." Brenna tilted her head apologetically and squeezed her hand.

"No you didn't. But thanks for trying to make me feel better." London gestured for Brenna's cigarette. She took a single drag then gave it back. "I won't ever be that stupid again."

"Maybe you need a vacation. We're both off this weekend. Let's drive out to Virginia Beach."

"I can't."

"Sure you can. You can ask Nurse Wendy to help Geneva with your grandma. Tyler and Libby can have some quality time with Seth."

"No way your husband is going to let you leave him all weekend with the kids."

"Come on, London. Let's do it," Brenna said. "His mom can come help take care of the kids."

London gritted her teeth and gasped for a deep, calming breath. "Will you stop with all the rainbows and sunshine shit? I said I can't go. Wick's daughter made another offer on Grammy's property and I have to make sure I get that taken care of so Geneva doesn't find out about it."

Clancy Wickerford, also known as Wick, was Vera's neighbor. He was the richest man in Coral Leaf and possibly all of West Virginia. London and Vera had been fighting with the Wickerford family since Clancy passed away over a year earlier. His daughter Alma-Rae wanted to buy Vera's lake-front property to build the luxury Pine Shadows Summer Resort.

"Not everybody is after your grandma's money. They aren't all greedy assholes," Brenna said.

"It's like Grammy says. If the mistakes of your past cast no shadow on your future decisions, you've been left in the dark," London said, gesturing for another drag from Brenna's cigarette. "Well, I've learned my lesson. I'm not trusting anyone when it comes to my Grammy."

"It is possible she is genuinely happy to meet her. Vera is a dear, good-hearted person. Maybe they really bonded."

"She's up to something. I just know it. She's another smooth-talker just like Brody. You should have seen her kissing up to Grammy and acting all sentimental."

"Your grandma is lucky to have you."

"No, I'm the lucky one," London insisted, noting the concern on her friend's face. "I'm sorry I snapped at you. You know I love you."

"Yea, I know. You just hate the rainbows and sunshine I have coming out of my ass." Brenna laughed.

"Stop it, Brenna." London laughed too. "I'm serious. You're my best friend."

"Shucks, cookie. You're my best friend too." Brenna nudged London with her elbow and smiled, then turned her attention to the car pulling into the parking lot. "That's why I hate to be the one to tell you that it's time to go back to work. Gotta' get ready for the lunch rush."

London replied with a lighthearted grumble, but she didn't mind going back to work. Brenna's tone was a signal that she needed to chill out and a few hours of busy work usually helped with that. Not that she really had any other choice. The vacation her friend suggested wasn't practical. Grammy's health was deteriorating too fast to leave her in a stranger's care. And that's exactly what Geneva was. A stranger.

Every day at eleven-thirty, a group of Pine Shadow construction workers arrived at the diner for lunch. Among the group was the construction foreman, Baxter Bruce. At barely 37 years old, his skin was wrinkled and leathery like an old man. His hands were always dirty and callused. He wore his dark blonde hair long and sported a shaggy beard. He was not London's usual type, but she was attracted to his rugged exterior and no-nonsense personality. He had his eye on her too and was relentless in his pursuit. He asked her for a date at least once a week. There were only two problems: she had no time for dating and he worked for the enemy.

Baxter arrived that day on schedule with two crew members, Hadley Morris and Denny Chapman, and an engineer named Marco Mora who was visiting from out of town. They sat at their same table in London's section. Baxter ordered his usual two glasses of sweet tea, a double-stacked BLT, and an order of onion rings. She introduced herself to the out-of-town stranger.

"Where are you from, Marco?"

"South Carolina," he said.

"South Carolina? What the heck are you doing all the way up here?"

Baxter interjected as Marco sipped from his freshly poured glass of tea. "We're getting ready to blast Mount Karma. We called in the expert."

London thrust her hip to the side, pointed her finger toward Baxter's face, and began scolding him. "Aren't you worried about bad karma blowing up the side of that mountain for a lousy hotel? You already chopped down all those beautiful trees."

"Is that why you won't go out with me, London?" He calmly grabbed the stainless steel tea pitcher from her hand and placed it on the table.

"Struck out again loser," Denny said. "I'm telling you man, you are chasing after the *wrong* sister."

In response, Baxter elbowed Denny and then angrily smacked the Mountaineers cap from head.

"What is he talking about?" London asked.

"Don't listen to a word that damn fool says," Baxter insisted.

Denny retrieved the cap and returned to the table still laughing. He extended his arm toward Marco and Hadley for a celebratory fist bump, but they didn't oblige. Either they were unimpressed by Denny's immaturity or they were intimidated by Baxter's angry expression.

"No, I'm serious. What the hell is going on? What do you know about my sister? She's been in town for one stinkin' day."

"We bumped into her at El Camino's last night," Hadley said.

"Fuckin' ay we did." Denny bragged. "I did all kinds of bumping into her last night. Got one hell of a hummer too."

Baxter took a swing at Denny's hat again, this time smacking his forehead with the back of his hand.

"What the hell, man?" Denny complained.

"Watch your damn mouth, Denny. You don't talk that way in front of a lady," Baxter said.

"Excuse me," she whispered, leaving the table to seek refuge In the kitchen.

London ducked into the walk-in freezer to hide out and cool off. She was embarrassed, disgusted, and angry. Denny Chapman was as slimy as they come. He was reasonably attractive, but lacked basic moral decency, especially when it came to his relationships with women. Based on her initial impression of Geneva, the two probably deserved each other. Nevertheless, a loser like Denny Chapman had no place in the Keller family circle. London cared nothing about Geneva's reputation, but her reckless behavior might reflect poorly on her and Grammy. Coral Leaf was not traditionally much of a rumor mill, but Denny Chapman had a big mouth and he could have something like this burning through town like a forest fire out of control; it wouldn't be the first time. London planned to confront Geneva and address the situation as soon as she got home from work that afternoon.

Baxter was waiting at the edge of the counter when London re-emerged from the kitchen. His presence startled her.

"What are you doing, Baxter?"

"Brenna wouldn't let me go back there to check on you," he said. His tone was uncharacteristically sincere. "I wanted to make sure you're okay."

"I just had to check on something," she said.

"That guy is a real douche."

"Oh, I know all about Denny Chapman. He's the town slut." London chuckled. "Or at least he was until Geneva showed up."

"Do you want me to fire him?" Baxter teased, leaning in and placing his hand on her shoulder.

"Yea, I do. And every other guy she sleeps with. That way you won't have a crew to build that damn resort and my grandma can keep her land."

"You know there's nothing I can do..."

London interrupted his sentence. "I know, Baxter. You're just doing your job. That doesn't make me feel any better." She pulled her shoulder away from his hand and picked up a water pitcher from the counter. "I have to get back to work."

"What if I told you I think your sister is white trash?"

She looked up at him and smiled. "Now that does make me feel better."

"Better enough for you to go out with me on Friday night?"

"No." She grinned at him and rolled her eyes.

"Saturday?" Baxter winked and bumped into her playfully.

"Baxter, I have to get back to work."

"I'm not gonna' quit asking until you say yes," he said.

"Go on. I'll bring your food when it's ready."

Baxter relented finally, but London couldn't ignore the difficulty she had rejecting him this time. Even Brenna commented about the smiling and playful banter. London denied her feelings to Brenna, but for the first time she was questioning her initial theory about Baxter. She had always believed his quest for her affections was motivated purely by primeval lust for the one woman he could not have. Suddenly, her mind was consumed with the notion he might truly care about her.

Chapter Two

Vera and London shared a secluded corner of Coral Leaf with the Wickerfords. Their only connection to their other neighbors was a narrow stretch of pavement – recently renamed the Pine Shadows Parkway – that led from the highway and down into their quiet valley. The parkway was flanked by groves of towering pine trees except for a small clearing where the roadway curved and began its steep descent down the Mount Karma hillside. This was London's first visibility to her grandmother's home. Her plans to confront Geneva about Denny Chapman were promptly derailed by the sight of an ambulance parked in front of Grammy's house. She feared the worst.

Cell phone service was spotty at best from this locale. With no way to reach Nurse Wendy, London panicked and began speeding down the mountain through the dark pine tree tunnel. Deep down she knew death would be a blessed relief for her grandmother, but she wasn't ready to let go. She didn't want her Grammy to die. Not yet. Would God really rob her of a chance to say goodbye to the most important person in her life? London cried up toward the heavens. "Please. Not again!"

The paramedics were still inside when London finally reached the house. With her car still running, she jumped from the driver's seat and charged into the house. Geneva greeted her frantically.

"Thank God you're here. I didn't know how to call you."

"What is going on? Where is Nurse Wendy?"

"I let her go home early."

London pushed past Geneva angrily and rushed toward the medics wheeling Vera down the hall. "Grammy! Grammy! Are you okay?"

Vera was conscious, but her oxygen mask prevented a response. One of the paramedics placed his hand on London's shoulder and gently nudged her away from the gurney. "Ma'am, your grandmother is stable, but we need to get her to the hospital."

"What happened? Is she going to be okay? Oh my God." London reached nervously for her grandmother as the other paramedic pushed the gurney past them. "I love you, Grammy."

"Why don't you ride with us to the hospital, ma'am," he said, gesturing toward Geneva standing several feet back. "You can come too, ma'am."

"No. No. How will we get back home? We need the car," London said.

"Okay. I'll ride in the ambulance. London will follow in the car," Geneva said. This suggestion infuriated London, but this was not the time to argue. Grammy needed help.

London followed the paramedics and her selfish sister out the door. The nearest hospital was about 30 minutes away in Connors Bluff. London and the ambulance made the trip this time in just over 20 minutes. Vera's cardiologist was already there awaiting her arrival. London wiped her teary eyes and promptly took charge of the insurance and admittance paperwork as her beloved grandmother disappeared behind the automatic emergency room doors. Geneva disappeared outside, presumably for a cigarette.

Once the necessary paperwork was completed, London took a seat in the busy waiting room. She had been watching the desk nurse escort each patient through the double doors into the treatment area of the hospital. She was desperate for answers about her grandmother's condition, but her stomach tightened each time the doors re-opened. She realized that at any moment Vera's cardiologist might return with dreaded news. London was wrenching her hands nervously. Geneva took the brunt of that anxiety as soon as she returned from outside.

"Have you heard anything yet?" Geneva asked.

"No!"

"I'm really worried."

"Why the hell did you send Wendy home? She could've died. It would have been all your fault."

"I didn't send her home. Her babysitter called and said Logan was sick. She seemed worried. I told her she could go," Geneva replied.

"Who is Logan?"

"Logan is her four-year-old son."

"I didn't know she had a son," London said, glancing at the young woman entering through the sliding doors with two small children.

Geneva sighed heavily. "Geez. She's been taking care of Grammy for almost two years and you didn't know she has a son. That's cold, London. Don't you ever just talk to the woman. She's really sweet and..."

"That's beside the point," London interrupted. "The fact is that you let her go home. What if Grammy had died?"

"She didn't die. I was there in the room with her. And you may think I'm too dumb to take care of her, but I'm smart enough to dial 911." Geneva plopped down on the sofa with her arms folded. "Now shut up and quit making a damn scene."

"I'm sorry."

"No you ain't, but I don't care. All I care about is Grammy getting better."

London *was* sorry for making a scene, but she meant what she said. Letting Wendy leave early was incredibly irresponsible and dangerous. She wanted to scold Geneva further on her pattern of reckless behavior, but instead just rolled her eyes and retreated to the opposite end of the waiting room. Fighting was a pointless waste of energy. She needed to stay strong to deal with the reality that her grandmother might never return home.

Vera was awake and alert by this time in the emergency ward and could sense her granddaughter's worry despite the distance between them. Their bond was that strong and always had been. When London was a little girl, Vera had the uncanny ability to read her thoughts, especially at night when the house was quiet. If the little girl was having a nightmare, Grammy would mysteriously be awake and right there by her side when London awoke. Clairvoyance would have been especially helpful for the two during this trying time, but London was always too skeptical about her grandmother's gift. She preferred to think of these incidents as coincidental or a miracle of strong motherly intuition. Either way, Vera hated knowing that her granddaughter needed her at that moment and that she wasn't able to be there. Instead, she was confined to a hospital bed awaiting test results and regretting that she had told the doctor about the nightmare that led to the episode.

Nurse Wendy kept Vera on a steady routine. Every day at two-thirty Vera got her second dose of heart medicine and a mild sleep aid. She liked to nap in the afternoon so that she would have enough energy to enjoy dinner with London when she got home from work; this was always their quality together time. Wendy usually helped the old woman to her room, turned on some classical music, and read to Vera until she fell asleep. Geneva helped on this day in Wendy's absence, delighting Vera with stories from her favorite movies and soap operas. She remembered Geneva kissing her hand and wrapping her arms tightly beneath her blankets for warmth, then she drifted into her dreams.

Vera told the doctor she was flying, soaring effortlessly in the wind and enjoying a magnificent view of her property. She saw birds nesting in the tree tops, the sunlight sparkling on the lake, and her dog Vienna chasing squirrels in the woods behind her house. Vera said as she pulled up to fly over Mount Karma, she encountered a cluster of white fluffy clouds. They were beautiful and inviting. She embraced one of the clouds and sank into it like a soft pillow. She remembered feeling very relaxed until the point she realized the cloud had consumed her body and head. She couldn't move and was finding it difficult to breathe. Vera swore she heard angels singing and repeatedly calling out to her. She also swore that Vienna was barking and chomping at the cloud to release her from its grip. That's when she awoke gasping for air.

The doctor didn't say much to Vera as the recounted the dream, but she overheard him tell the nurse he was concerned about brain damage. He expressed the same concern to her granddaughters when he finally joined them in the waiting room nearly 90 minutes later.

London raced to the doctor's side, competing with her sister to get there first. "Is she okay? Please tell me she's going to be okay."

"She is stable for now."

"You said she's stable," London said, nibbling nervously on her thumb nail. "Does that mean she can come home with me tonight?"

"Well, her oxygen stats are very low and she seems confused and disoriented. That raises concerns that her brain may have been deprived of oxygen for a period of time during this episode."

"What happened?" Geneva asked. "Was it another stroke or something?"

"The EKG shows no signs of a heart attack and there aren't any immediate signs of a stroke, but given her history we need to monitor her closely," he said. "Especially since we're not sure what caused the episode."

"How long?" Geneva asked.

"At least overnight," he said. "The nurse is going to make arrangements for you to meet with Rachel from Elmwood Nursing Home and Hospice care in the morning. She will..."

"Hospice care? Is that really..." London gasped. "necessary?" London wasn't ready to lose Grammy, but she deserved a quick, painless departure from this world. Hospice care at a nursing home sounded like torture and she was not prepared for any discussion on that topic.

"I know this is very difficult. But as I've said before, your grandmother's condition will continue to deteriorate. I really feel that 24 hour care would be best for her."

London ignored the doctor's recommendation and edged forward toward the emergency ward doors. "Can I see her?"

"Well, she was having some anxiety so we gave her something to help her relax. She is probably resting now, but I will take you girls back to see her. You can visit while admissions works on getting her transferred upstairs."

The girls rushed to their grandmother's bedside, but neither said a word to her or to each other. Vera was sleeping as the doctor predicted. She sensed the girls' arrival, but the sedative prevented her from waking for more than just a few seconds. Her voice was frail and her words were jumbled, but she tried offering reassurance that God wasn't ready for her yet. London didn't believe her and she argued with the ICU nurse when she insisted they leave for the night. Her breathing was labored and shallow. London didn't want to risk leaving Grammy to die alone in some hospital. Needless to say, London lost that argument and needless to say, she was angry.

In what was becoming her usual fashion, she lashed out at Geneva in the car on the way home. An innocent question about Vera's insurance unleashed a blast of raw emotion from the tips of London's toes.

"This is all your fault, you stupid bitch!"

"What? Wait a minute."

"None of this would have happened if you hadn't come here. Now Grammy is dying. And it's your damn fault. Just like with mom."

"What the hell are you talking about?"

"She and Shawn had to go out in the middle of a rain storm to buy more diapers for you. That's probably why Grammy couldn't keep you. She probably hates you too."

"Fuck you," Geneva yelled. "You fucking bitch!"

Geneva swung her arm and whacked London hard across the face and body. The impact forced the steering wheel out of London's hands and the car swerved out of control into the other lane. London scrambled to regain control, then pulled the car over to the side of the road and stopped.

"Are you crazy! Are you trying to kill us too?"

Geneva slipped out of her seatbelt and lunged toward London, forcing her arm firmly against her throat. "Don't you ever talk to me like that again. Ever! I have just as much right to be here as you do and I'm not going anywhere."

London finally managed to push her away.

"And that shit you said about Grammy is a lie. I asked Grammy why she gave me up and she said it was because she couldn't handle a baby and *you.* You were too much of a handful."

"Shut up," London grumbled.

"And she knew a cute baby like me..."

"Shut up!" London screamed this time, and pushed Geneva forcefully against the passenger door.

"...would have no trouble getting adopted. And you'd be all sad and lonely in an orphanage forever."

"Get the hell out of my car."

"No," Geneva said, folding her arms across her chest. "Take me home. And tomorrow morning we're going to talk to that nursing home lady. You're gonna' stop being selfish and let them take care of Grammy and get her what she deserves."

"I don't know who the hell you think you are, but..."

"I'm her granddaughter," Geneva interrupted. "That means I get the same amount of say so as you do about Grammy."

"Whatever." London shook her head and turned away from Geneva's intimidating stare.

"Not whatever. I have rights!"

"You've been here 24 hours and you think you have the right to tell me how to take care of my Grammy."

London turned back to face Geneva and awaited a response. Geneva said nothing; she wouldn't even look at her. London let out a quiet, victorious chuckle then put the car back in gear and continued their journey home. Neither girl said anything until they arrived back at the house. London entered the house assuming that the argument was over. That's when Geneva cornered her in the foyer between the staircase landing and the antique writing desk along the adjacent wall.

"Now you agree that tomorrow we're going to talk to the nursing home lady like Doc said. Right?" Geneva's fist was clinched and pressed firmly against London's rib cage.

"You just want to put her in a nursing home so you don't have to feel guilty while you sleep your way through the men in this town."

Geneva's only response was laughter.

"I know all about you and Denny Chapman at El Caminos. And I know all about you giving him a blow job in the men's restroom." London shuttered and pretended to gag. "Could you be more skanky?"

Geneva thrust her weight against London and taunted her with a wicked stare. "I'm skanky? Ya' know I heard some things about you too."

"Get away from me." London pushed Geneva with all her strength and escaped toward the kitchen.

"I know all about you and the lawn care guy."

"Who? Travis? What about him?"

"Wendy said she caught you two getting it on in the bedroom one day."

"That's not a secret," London grunted. "What? Did you and your new best friend Wendy sit around and talk about me all day? She's here to take care of Grammy. Not to gossip."

"Why does it bother you that I'm friends with her?"

"It doesn't." London passed through the kitchen toward her bedroom at that end of the house. Geneva was following closely behind.

"I think you're scared she's going to take my side and that she's going to help me get Grammy into the nursing home."

"No, I'm not worried about that." London opened the laundry room door and peeked in to find Vienna. She could hear her barking, but she hadn't greeted her like she usually did.

"Where is my dog? I swear if you did something to Vienna…"

"I locked her in your bedroom. The damn thing bit me."

London chuckled and whispered under her breath as she continued down the hall to her bedroom. "Good dog."

"I'm right behind you. I heard that."

"Good. I hope she took a shit in your bed too." London really amused herself with that insult.

"That's very funny," Geneva scowled. "You know, you can judge me all you want, but there isn't nothing wrong with what I did with Denny. We was just having fun."

"Isn't nothing? We was? You should have spent more time in English class and less time under the bleachers." London entered her room without answering Geneva's question. She tried to close and lock the door behind her, but Geneva pushed her way in. She could see her sister in the mirror above her dresser; she was leaned back against the door frame smiling and seemingly admiring her own reflection. Vienna cowered behind the bed and growled – behavior that suggested she was afraid of Geneva. "Did you hit my dog?"

"No, I didn't hit your stupid dog."

London turned abruptly and pointed her finger at Geneva's face. "Get this straight! If you lay one finger on her, I will kick your ass out of this house. You'll be gone faster than your underwear comes off on a first date." She lifted Vienna from the floor. In the comfort of her arms, she started barking again and snarling her teeth. "Oh, that's right Vienna. She's a whore. She probably doesn't wear any underwear."

Geneva leaned forward from her resting place in the door frame. "At least I didn't almost marry a conman."

London's triumphant, arrogant smile disappeared. "Get out of my room."

"Did I touch a nerve?

"You shouldn't be talking about things you don't understand."

"Oh, but I do understand. I know all about you and Brody Danbrook and how you almost cost Grammy her life savings."

"I am not having this conversation with you. Now get the hell out of my room!"

Geneva continued her rant, unthreatened by the hatred in London's eyes. "You should know half the town thinks you were in on that scheme. You just got cold feet when Grammy got sick."

"Shut up!" London felt as though every blood vessel in her face was bursting as she screamed.

"Hey, I'm not saying I believe it. Just repeating what everybody else is saying."

"One more word and I swear I am going to..." London stopped herself from finishing the sentence. Geneva's self-righteous demeanor had infuriated her. The intensity of her anger was frightening. For a split second she pictured hurling something sharp and heavy across the room, causing a bloody scene when the object struck the uneducated, dime-store whore in the forehead.

Geneva remained unexplainably calm and impervious to her sister's threat. "You're going to do what? Hit me?"

London said nothing more. She knew Geneva was trying to provoke a fight. She probably wanted London to punch her to gain sympathy with her new friends and to recruit support for her mission to put Grammy in a nursing home. London was too smart for that. She pushed past Geneva and left the room to take the dog for her walk. This time Geneva did not follow.

London and Vienna followed their usual route through the wooded back acres toward the lake. They walked the path Grampy Keller had cleared with his tractor years earlier and crossed the hand-built wooden bridge over Ripley Blue Creek. As usual, they stopped for a rest at the lake-side clubhouse and boat dock her grandfather constructed just three years before he passed away. London liked the spot because of her fond memories with Grampy. Vienna seemed more enamored with the pile of boat seat cushions in the corner. She needed to rest after such a long walk. London needed some time alone to deal with the gravity of her grandmother's health situation. She opened the window's storm hatch, lounged back on one of the cushioned deck chairs, and admired her view of the moonlit mountain top.

Vera had already survived longer than any doctor expected, but that fact was neither comforting nor worrisome. There was a chance that the doctors were completely wrong about Vera's condition and prognosis; maybe the stroke had not done as much damage as they suspected. On the other hand, the timing of her sudden, drastic decline definitely had London questioning whether God had just been granting Grammy a short reprieve until she met Geneva. The debate about moving Grammy to a nursing home was pointless when she considered the possibility that she might never leave the hospital at all. London decided to return to the house just in case the hospital called overnight.

Geneva was asleep on Grammy's bed by the time London and Vienna returned to the house just after midnight. The scene seemed quite pretentious. Geneva was snuggled in Grammy's quilt with an old family photo album opened beside her. There was a wad of Kleenex tissues on the nightstand and another stack of photo albums and scrapbooks piled up on the floor beside the bed. London was not convinced by Geneva's pose as the grieving granddaughter. Furthermore, she was disgusted by her obvious lack of concern for all that London and Grammy had been through together.

London was only five years old when her mother died, but she remembered the funeral. She remembered the fragrant flowers that decorated the church altar and the framed photo displayed beside the urn. They scattered Sicily's ashes in the lake with a heart-shaped wreath made of red roses right where Mount Karma's peak reflected in the water – the spot Sicily always referred to as the heart of the lake or "Le Cœur du Lac". That was the first time she ever saw Grammy cry. The only other time she saw her cry was when they returned 13 years later to that same spot to scatter Grampy's ashes. For the 14 years since, she and Grammy only had each other. London knew what was best for her grandmother; she wasn't going to let Geneva coast into town and take over.

Chapter Three

After three days and a series of inconclusive test results, Vera's insurance company was pressing for her release from the hospital. The cardiologist was reluctant to let Vera go home and London refused to consider the nursing home as an option; Grammy had made her wishes very clear. They did, however, reach a compromise about 24-hour nursing care and an in-home hospice case worker. Vera and the girls met with the case worker after London's work shift on Tuesday afternoon. The doctor signed her release a short time later and London took her grandmother home. Geneva drove separately and planned to meet them back at the house.

Losing her eyesight had given Vera a different perspective and new appreciation for her surroundings. She couldn't see the beautiful white and lavender wildflowers that lined the hospital parkway, but could still enjoy their fragrance with every breath. She knew that was an aspect of the journey that both granddaughters probably took for granted. She sensed they were taking each other for granted too. The tension and angst were as obvious as the smell of cigarettes on Geneva's clothes. Vera decided to use this time alone with London to offer her advice.

"I know these last few days have been really hard on you, sweetheart."

"It's okay, Grammy." London squeezed her grandmother's hand then replaced her grip on the steering wheel. "I am so thankful you're out of that hospital. I've missed you so much. And I know Vienna has too."

"I know. It will be good to sleep in my own bed again," Vera replied. "But I was talking about things being tough since Geneva got here. I really wish the two of you could work out the troubles between you."

"It's fine, Grammy. I promise."

"No, it's not fine. You girls barely speak to each other. You behave like you can't stand to be in the same room with one another." Vera reached for London's hand again. "I know you aren't happy about her being here, London. But she thinks you hate her."

"I don't hate her." London shook her head feeling annoyed and slightly ashamed.

"Dear, she told me what you said to her. That you blame her for me getting sick and for your momma's death. Honey, these things aren't anybody's fault. They're just part of life and..."

London interrupted to defend herself. "I was angry. I didn't really mean what I said to her."

"Don't you think you should apologize?"

"She said some pretty awful things to me too. Did she tell you that?" London felt stupid for not realizing Geneva would go behind her back. Surely the story she shared was a self-serving, distorted version of what really happened.

"She told me everything, sweetheart." Vera paused to take a deep breath.

"Maybe you should rest, Grammy, and catch your breath. We'll have plenty of time to talk about this later. I don't want you to overdo it."

No matter how much London wanted to dodge this difficult topic, Vera knew she had to somehow mend the situation between the two girls. The need was critical because although the doctor's response at the hospital kept Vera from telling anyone, her night terrors were continuing and becoming more vivid and intense. Every time she fell asleep she was exposed to horrific images of dark shadows, fire, dragons, sharks, and death. The nightmares had changed her outlook on her health and longevity and she no longer felt assured she would be there to protect her beloved granddaughters. They would need to protect each other.

"You can't always count on later. There are no guarantees," Vera responded.

"Please don't talk about that." London swallowed hard to choke back her tears. "You're fine. All the tests came back fine and you're going home. And..."

"Geneva is family. She's your only family once I'm gone. I'm just asking you to open your heart a little, London. I know you're trying to protect yourself. And me. But you have to let people in." Vera paused for another deep breath. "I don't know how much time I have left."

"Don't worry. I'm going to take good care of you." Hearing fear in her grandmother's voice made it hard to harness her emotions. A lone tear streaked down London's cheek as she straightened Vera's oxygen hose and adjusted the blanket in her lap. "And I promise to make peace with Geneva."

"That's all I ask." Vera smiled and lifted London's hand to kiss it. "You're a good girl, London. You make me so proud."

London committed to giving Geneva a second chance for her grandmother's sake. Neither ever officially apologized, but Geneva seemed to embrace the opportunity to start over. London began partnering with her on Grammy's morning ritual and the three of them started eating dinner together in the evenings. They rarely saw each other beyond that. With 24-hour nursing care, Grammy had encouraged London to return to work during the day at the diner. Geneva got a weekend bartending job at El Camino's and during the week usually met up with Denny and her new friends after Vera went to bed. Almost two weeks had passed without a single conflict between the two girls. Grammy was pleased.

Those same two weeks had also passed without Baxter asking London for a date. He was overdue and London was a little disappointed. Grammy's words that day on the way home from the hospital had a profound effect. She wasn't the type to need a man to take care of her, but London didn't like the idea of being alone through such a difficult loss. Geneva was surely enjoying the spoils of male companionship. London deserved to do the same. When Baxter lingered at his table alone after lunch on Friday, she hoped he planned to ask again for a date.

"Do you want another refill?" she asked, holding up the stainless steel tea pitcher.

Baxter smiled. "No. I wanted to see if you can take your break now. Maybe go outside for a cigarette."

"I really shouldn't leave..."

"It's important," he insisted. "There's something I really need to tell you about."

Baxter wasn't usually shy about propositioning her in front of other people, so London was confused and curious.

"Brenna, can you cover for me? I'm going to take my break now," she said.

"Sure." Brenna shrugged. She seemed equally confused.

London followed Baxter outside. She retrieved her cigarettes from the car and joined him where he was standing near the bed of his truck. His facial expression was different, more serious than London had ever seen.

"Have you seen Denny Chapman lately? He showed up drunk a couple mornings ago, complaining that Geneva dumped him. Alma-Rae fired him. "

London gasped. She felt no sympathy for Denny, but the news was shocking. Denny was a distant relative to the Wickerford family. He had been on the construction project from the beginning.

"The guy is a loser, but I did kind of feel bad for him."

"No. I haven't seen him," she said, staring at Baxter curiously. Surely he hadn't called her outside just to tell her that Geneva and Denny had broken up.

"I guess I should get to the point here," Baxter said, obviously noticing the puzzled look on her face. "I saw your sister out at the site today. She and Alma-Rae were by the pool, looking very chummy and drinking some kind of frozen cocktails."

"Geneva and Alma-Rae Wickerford? Chummy?"

"Denny said Alma-Rae calls her Evie. He told me that she'd used him to get her foot in the door with Alma-Rae, but I didn't believe it until I saw them together today. I guess they hang out together all the time now."

"I knew we couldn't trust that bitch!" London lifted her hands to her face and began involuntarily grinding her finger tips up and down from her bangs to her brow. "Dammit!"

"I didn't want you to get upset, but you needed to know."

London's physical reaction was mild in comparison to the raging thoughts going through her mind. She felt as though she'd been struck by a wrecking ball, lifted from the ground, and left dangling without solid ground beneath her feet.

"I can help you," Baxter offered. "I can make sure they don't..."

"No. No. I don't need any help." London glanced at him, noting the sincerity in his eyes. This conversation was far from what she expected, but so was his willingness to challenge anyone in the Wickerford family. His involvement could cost him his job. She wondered what incentive she'd given for his loyalty. "Why did you tell me that? You didn't have to."

"I know I come across most the time as a hard ass, but I am capable of being a nice guy. I care about what happens to you and your grandma. I know you really love her."

"With all my heart."

"That's probably why I'm so crazy about you. You have a good heart."

London shook her head modestly.

"Besides that. You are smart and strong and sexy. And you make me laugh with all the clever jabs at me and my crew. I like a woman who can stand up to a group of tough brutes like us. But it's tough to be strong when people are doing you wrong behind your back. You deserve to know."

"Thank you," she said. "For the compliments and for telling me about Geneva. I promise not to let her know it was you who told me."

Baxter took a final drag from his cigarette then tossed it onto the gravel parking lot. "I don't care if you tell her."

"I don't want her to say anything to Alma-Rae. I don't want you to lose your job."

"There are plenty of other jobs," he said. "That might be the only way I ever get you to change your mind about going out on a date with me."

"Baxter, I..."

He placed his hand gently against her lips. "Don't say anything. I'm just going to go now."

London didn't get a chance to say anything more. He took off quickly in his truck and left her to contemplate her next step. She knew she had to confront Geneva. She also knew she wanted to avoid making trouble for Baxter. She just wasn't exactly sure how to start the conversation without mentioning his name or what he had seen at the Wickerford's house.

Brenna was wiping down the counter when London came back inside. She was obviously interested in the outcome of her conversation with Baxter. "That's not the facial expression I expected."

"He didn't ask me out. He told me that he saw Geneva over at the Wickerford's estate."

"What was she doing over there?"

The other day-shift waitress, Claudia Plumm, was bussing a nearby table and decided to butt in on their conversation. "She and Alma-Rae are like best friends now."

"What are you talking about? How do you know?" Brenna asked.

"Marlene Sullivan told me. She said she heard it from Denny's sister Chloe."

"I wonder who else knows about this," London said. She took the wash bin from Claudia and handed it across the counter to Brenna.

"A lot of people," Claudia replied, gesturing for London to pass a squirt bottle and sponge. "I was at El Camino's last night and Denny was telling everybody about how she dumped him. He says he thinks Geneva and Alma-Rae are lesbians."

Brenna laughed. "That's what all guys think when they get dumped."

"No. You know what. He may be right," London said.

There were no customers, so London sat down at the table Claudia was cleaning. She gestured for the other girls to join her.

"What do you mean?" Brenna asked.

"Grammy told me when Geneva first called that she thought she was gay. She said she kept talking about how she shared an apartment with her girlfriend Adrienne. But when Geneva hooked up so quick with Denny, I just assumed Grammy had misunderstood."

"Well, Alma-Rae has been married and divorced three times. Maybe she decided to switch teams," Claudia said.

"But if Geneva is gay, why would she sleep with Denny?" Brenna asked. "I mean, come on. Look at her. She's gorgeous. She could probably have her choice of men in this town and she picks Denny Chapman?"

London leaned forward and rested her elbows on the table. "Denny told Baxter that he thought Geneva had used him to get to Alma-Rae. Maybe she did."

"You should look her up on Facebook when you get home," Brenna suggested. "See if you can find out about this girlfriend Adrienne."

"I don't have Facebook. We don't even have internet."

"I'll do it then. And I'll let you know what I find out."

"I think I'm just going to ask her. I just hope it doesn't turn into another big fight," London said. "I promised Grammy I would try to get along with her."

"This is different," Brenna said. "You're just trying to make sure she isn't screwing you over."

"I'll figure something out." London agreed with Brenna's statement, but was still unsure how to address the situation without breaking her promise. She decided on her way home that evening, that perhaps the best approach was to talk with Grammy first.

Vera was sleeping when London got home. Geneva had left already for work. Vienna was waiting anxiously by the back door. London took the dog for a short walk to relieve herself, then joined Grammy and her nurse in the bedroom. She kissed her grandmother on the forehead then greeted Wendy, who was relaxing in the rocking chair by the window.

"How did she do today?" London asked quietly.

"She slept a lot again today and wouldn't eat or drink anything. I also had to put another blanket on her bed. She was cold."

London glanced at her grandmother again, sleeping still and peacefully in her bed. Her hands were folded at her chest as if she was praying. London tried to ignore the thin, frailty of her grandmother's shape beneath her blankets, but she could not deny her concern. Vera had always been cold-natured, but the temperature had soared near 90 degrees that day and the afternoon sun had done a good job warming her bedroom.

"Is it chills? Does she have a fever?"

"Her temperature was 99.8 last time I checked. That's only slightly elevated."

"What do you think it is?"

"I'm not her doctor, London. But I did make a call to the caseworker and asked for hospice visit in the morning."

Worry and tension stretched across London's brow. "Is that really necessary? Already?"

"There's no way to know for certain. Miss Vera is a fighter. We both know that. Sometimes the body just isn't as strong as the spirit."

Fear overwhelmed London and she continued pressing for a more definitive explanation or prognosis, but Wendy declined to say any more. She hugged London for the first time since their meeting and told her to pray. London did pray. She prayed for peace for her grandmother's beautiful soul. She prayed for strength to let go.

Nurse Wendy stayed with London until six o'clock when the other nurse, Judy, came to relieve her from duty. When Geneva got home from work at the bar early Saturday morning, Judy helped London break the news about Vera's condition. She decided not to confront Geneva about her recent visits to the Wickerford estate. Her relationship with Alma-Rae seemed far less important than ensuring a calm, loving environment for Grammy. Even if Geneva's motive was greed, the house and her entire estate were already designated in the will to be shared by both girls equally. Fighting seemed petty at this point. Instead, London spent the early morning hours with her sister sharing pictures and stories about Grammy. Her company was surprisingly comforting.

Vera woke briefly just after sunrise. She had been dreaming about angels sent to take her home. She knew this dream was a message from God letting her know he was ready for her. It was time to tell her girls goodbye. She tried to reach for her bell, but was too weak to lift her arm from beneath the blankets.

"I'm right here. You don't need the bell," London said, kissing her face just as she had done every morning for the past two years.

Vera tried to speak. Tears glistened in the corners of her eyes as London caressed the soft, gray curls from her brow.

"It's okay, Grammy. You need to save your strength," London whispered. "Geneva and I are both here."

"Everything will be alright," Geneva said.

Vera closed her eyes again and fell back to sleep with her granddaughter's holding her hands.

Judy smiled sympathetically at the girls. "She loves you very, very much. She's told me herself how much she loves you. She is very lucky to have you here by her side."

"She told you that?" Geneva asked.

"Yes she did."

London said nothing. She was touched by the nurse's kindness, but didn't feel like she needed affirmation about how her grandmother felt. For the last two years, "I love you" had been the first words Vera said every day and the last words she said every night as London tucked her beneath her covers and shut out the light. Even though she was too weak at this point to say the words, London's connection to her grandmother was finally strong enough to transcend words. She felt surrounded by her grandmother's spirit and love.

The hospice nurse confirmed, upon her arrival, that there were signs Vera's body was starting to shut down. Her heart rate was slowing and her respirations were shallow and somewhat intermittent. She was fading and would likely drift away in her sleep in the coming days. From the moment London heard this news, she and Vienna barely left Grammy's side. When she slept at all, she slept in the bedroom on an overstuffed lounger in the corner. The dog slept on the carpet beside the bed. Geneva, on the other hand, followed the nurse's advice. There was no way to predict how much time Vera had left; the girls needed to allow themselves breaks from the physical and emotional stress in order to keep up their strength. She didn't judge Geneva's choice to leave the room for food, sleep, or fresh air. She just knew she couldn't live with herself if she missed a single breath, a single murmur, or a single minute of Grammy's remaining life. Grammy was London's source of strength.

Vera died on Tuesday evening. London and Geneva were both by her side.

Chapter Four

"Thankful are eyes that weep with sorrow. They are eyes that once saw beauty. Blessed is the heart that aches for the love and joy it once knew. Hopeful is the soul where darkness casts a shadow. Beyond the sadness, behind the grief, the sunshine still awaits."

Reverend Walker bowed his head and prayed as London and Geneva together scattered their Grammy's ashes into the lake and placed the wreath of white roses to mark her final resting place. Geneva wept dramatically. Tears dampened the corners of London's eyes, but her heart was oddly at peace in that moment. Lake Amethyst glistened more brightly on that morning, like the beautiful purple jewel for which it was named. London knew the reason. Vera's spirit had finally been reunited with her husband and daughter; all three spirits were smiling. London smiled too as she pictured her Grammy and Grampy holding Sicily together in their arms for the first time in 28 years. Le Coeur du Lac was the ideal place for such a loving reunion. London knew she would never look at her mother's painting the same way ever again.

The reverend's words still echoed in London's mind as she greeted the fellowship of friends and neighbors gathered at Vera's house after the memorial service on Saturday morning. She agreed completely with the sentiment, but had difficulty reconciling the words with how she felt in those days following her grandmother's death. Sorrow cast such a dark shadow in her world – darkness that seemed impenetrable by even the brightest sunlight. London thanked each guest for paying their respects, but spoke very little beyond that. Her Grammy was gone and no amount of sympathy or kindness could soften the edge of that devastating reality.

Geneva, on the other hand, seemed to thrive as the center of attention. She cried dramatically about the short time she'd gotten to know Vera and bragged about how desperately she tried to save her life. London was sickened by the pretentious display, but was too depressed to fight. She and Brenna withdrew from the crowd and took a walk with the dog around the property.

"Calvin's tribute to your Grammy was beautiful," Brenna said. Though he was long-retired from the church, London had asked her boss to officiate Vera's service.

"He loved her too."

"Everybody did. She was a wonderful woman, London."

"You can't imagine how much I miss her. Already. I actually got up yesterday morning at 6:30 and walked into her room to wake her up. I forgot she was gone – just for a minute. It just about killed me."

"That's gotta' be hard."

"I hadn't cried very much at all. Not even on Tuesday when the angels took her. But yesterday I completely fell apart. I bet I was in there for an hour, laying on the floor and crying so hard I couldn't catch my breath. My grandmother was the most amazing woman in the world. How could I forget that she was gone? I was so mad at myself."

"Your brain was just probably trying to protect you. Maybe like one of those defense mechanism things. Reality was too harsh, so you had to block it out or something."

"I'm sure that's part of it," London said. She tugged Vienna's leash to warn her away from Grammy's hibiscus bushes and the bees swarming about. "I know this is going to sound crazy, but I still feel like she's here."

"That's not crazy," Brenna replied. "That's not crazy at all. She'll always be with you."

"There's been a couple times I even felt like she was watching me. Even Vienna got a little spooked."

"I didn't think you believed in that kind of stuff."

London shrugged. "I don't. But I did say 'I love you' just in case."

"She knew how much you loved her. You would have given your life for your Grammy, London. I know that. And I'm sure she knew that too," Brenna said, wrapping her arm around London's shoulder. "I feel so bad for you. Everybody does. Baxter too. He told me to let you know he was thinking about you today."

"That was really nice."

"We're all very sad."

London nodded her head. "Apparently not as sad as my sister. Did you see her in there? Alma-Rae was practically cradling her like a baby. Evie has been staying over at the Wickerford house since Grammy died."

"I thought maybe they were lovers or something."

London shrugged and looked down at Vienna sniffing the grass. She wanted to comment about Alma-Rae's nerve showing up at a memorial service for the woman whose home she was trying to steal away, but she didn't have the energy. She said nothing.

"Seriously," Brenna continued. "I checked out her Facebook page the other night after we talked. There's a picture of her and another girl looking very chummy, if ya' know what I mean."

London crouched down to pet Vienna on the head. "That's probably her old roommate Adrienne."

"Maybe. Her profile was locked so I couldn't see anything else."

"I don't think she's gay. I think she's just looking for a new mommy," London said, "Anyway, it doesn't matter if she's gay or bi or straight or whatever. Half this place is hers now. Grammy put it in her will. She can do whatever she wants."

Brenna stopped walking. "So you're just going to give up?"

"I told you. There is nothing I can do. It's in Grammy's will."

"Then contest it."

"Please, Brenna! Don't start with me about this. I'm upset enough as it is already."

Brenna stood motionless and stared in disbelief.

"I need to go back into the house now." London tugged lightly on Vienna's leash. "Come on, Vienna. Let's go get you a drink. Momma needs one too."

Nurse Wendy stopped London on her way to the kitchen and handed her a pink envelope with embossed roses on the edge. She recognized the stationary as that Grammy kept in the antique desk in the front foyer. Before her stroke she frequently wrote letters to London using that stationary. London worked six days a week at that time and typically only saw her grandmother on Sundays when they attended church together. Grammy didn't have a house phone back then either, so she sent mail – one or two letters during the week to tell her about her little flower garden or her baking, crocheting, and craft projects for the church charity fundraisers. London loved that.

"Did you take that from my grandmother's desk?" she asked accusingly.

"Yes. She asked me to write down what she said," Wendy said. She sniffled, obviously distraught over Vera's passing. "She wanted her girls to know one more time how much she loved you."

Confusion disarmed London of her prior judgment. She took the letter from Wendy's hand and traced her finger along the decorative vines embossed along the edge. "Thank you."

"I'm very sorry for your loss, London. I cared for your grandmother very much."

"Thank you," she repeated, this time in a barely audible whisper.

Wendy said nothing more. She walked away with tears in her eyes, gently patting London on the back as she passed by.

Geneva was already reading her letter aloud to everyone in the room, revealing Vera's words about the heartache she and Grampy felt when they kissed their little baby granddaughter goodbye for the last time. She remembered Geneva was wearing pajamas with "Funshine Bear" on the front because that was Sicily's nickname for her little girl. That sunny Care Bear, according to Grammy's letter, remained a symbol of hope that Geneva was enjoying a better life because of that heart wrenching decision. Geneva cried out and practically collapsed into Alma-Rae's arms as others around her tried to provide comfort. Brenna rolled her eyes. London disappeared into her bedroom feeling sick. She wasn't reading her letter, not out loud and not on this day. She tucked the envelope into her purse then ventured toward the kitchen as originally planned.

London's broken spirit craved straight vodka, but she added enough orange juice to hopefully fool her guests. She remembered her first two screwdrivers, but everything else about that day was a complete blur. She awoke with the worst ever hangover. Her bedroom floor was littered with crumpled paper and empty liquor bottles and beer cans. Her room reeked of urine where Vienna relieved herself on the floor and vomit from the plastic waste basket beside the bed. Geneva's laughter was barging through her seemingly paper-thin bedroom walls and pounding her head like a three year old on a piano. She desperately needed to stop the noise, but realized yelling at her sister might call attention to the embarrassing remnants of her drunken stupor. She wasn't sure she'd even be able to speak anyway. Her throat felt like she had swallowed the desert. A long, hot shower drowned the evidence of London's self-destructive behavior, but did little for the disgrace she saw in her mirrored reflection. What had she done to herself? Grammy would not have approved.

Geneva was in the living room cleaning up empty pizza boxes and beer cans when London finally emerged to confront her. She was alone, but the room's disarray suggested she'd spent the previous night entertaining. In addition to the beer cans and trash, the sofa was pushed back against the front picture window and replaced by the dining room table and 3 of the chairs. The fourth chair was laying on its side with a broken leg.

"What the hell?"

Geneva turned to face her, seemingly startled by London's entry into the room. "You look like death."

"What are you doing here? Hadn't you practically moved in at the Wickerford mansion?"

Geneva grunted, stuffing pizza boxes into a trash bag. "What does it look like I'm doing? I'm cleaning up your mess."

"My mess? What are you talking about?" London couldn't deny that she'd been drunk, but she was never a partier. No amount of alcohol would have provoked such behavior.

"I guess you had one hell of a party last night."

"I did no such thing! I drank too much last night after Grammy's service, but..."

"London," Geneva interrupted. "Grammy's service was three days ago. It's Tuesday."

"You are such a liar."

"I am not a liar. You didn't show up for work at the diner this morning. Brenna got worried and came to check on you. She found you passed out on the front porch... Naked."

"That's a damn lie!" London folded her arms across her chest and gazed aimlessly about the room trying to recall exactly what had happened in those past 72 hours. She remembered nothing. She hoped desperately that she was lying.

Brenna emerged from the kitchen with Vienna on a leash by her side. "Quit screwing with her, Geneva."

"Aw, come on." Geneva chuckled.

"See, I knew you were lying." London kicked the trash bag next to Geneva's feet and shot her a dirty look.

"Well, she was lying about the naked part, but I was worried about you. I've been trying to call you for three days."

"Three days? You mean it's really Tuesday?" Thoughts were swirling in London's head almost making her dizzy. Perhaps the alcohol had affected her concept of time.

"You wouldn't answer the phone. I stood here for fifteen minutes ringing the doorbell earlier. I had to go find Geneva to get the key."

"Oh my God!"

"Who were you partying with?" Brenna asked.

London gasped. She plopped backward onto the couch and buried her face in her hands. "I don't remember partying at all."

"And you had the nerve to judge me," Geneva scowled. "I bet it was the guy who mows the grass."

"Stop it. Don't make things worse," Brenna said. She sat down next to London and squeezed her leg. Vienna joined them on the couch and curled up close to her side. "Do you want me to take you to talk to somebody? Or maybe to see the doctor?"

London lifted her head and replied abruptly. "I don't need a doctor. I don't want anybody to see me like this."

"Maybe it was your ex-boyfriend. What's his name? Brody?" Geneva cackled and stomped her feet, clearly amused by the idea.

London buried her head again.

Brenna got angry. "Geneva, get the hell out of here! Go back to your rich-bitch mansion on the hill. I'm sure Alma-Rae is waiting to give you your bath."

"Jealous?" Geneva threw her hip to the side and glared back at Brenna, licking her lips.

"You are sick."

"Will you both just shut the hell up?" London roared. "My freakin' head feels like it's going to explode."

"I'm sorry, honey." Brenna got up from the sofa, crossed the room, and lifted the black trash bag Geneva had been stuffing. "You can go now. I will take care of this mess."

Geneva shook her head. "Nah. I think I better stick around and make sure she doesn't do any more damage to my house."

London glared angrily at her.

"Oops. I mean our house."

"This is Grammy's house."

"Grammy is dead," Geneva responded coldly. "She left the house to us. And if you keep throwing these wild parties we ain't gonna' get no decent money for it."

"You are such a greedy bitch!" London sprang to her feet ready for a physical confrontation with her sister, but her sudden movement made the room spin again.

Vienna launched herself onto the floor and started barking as London struggled back to her resting place. Brenna scolded Geneva with an ugly facial expression, then crossed the room to retrieve the dog.

"Come on, London. You can stay at my place for a few days."

"No. No. I can't do that."

"Yes you can. We've got the extra bedroom for when Seth's mom visits. There's plenty of room. Vienna can come too. The kids would love having a dog to play with. And I'll enjoy having an excuse for my mother-in-law not to visit for fourth of July."

London gritted her teeth and tried again to refuse her friend's invitation. "Brenna, I can't leave her here with the house. There's no telling what she'll do. She'll probably try to sell it right out from under me."

"She can't do that. You told me yourself. Now, let's get your things. I'm not taking no for an answer." With a bit more encouragement from Brenna, London finally complied with her request.

Geneva smiled victoriously and waved from the front porch as London and Brenna drove away. London was hardly a trusting person to begin with, but she feared the worst leaving her grandmother's belongings in the hands of someone like Geneva. Her clever jab about London's supposed wild party made her motives quite clear; Geneva was trying to discredit her and make her look like the bad guy. Brenna assured her that the people of Coral Leaf were too smart for that.

Whispering Trail was the name of the gravel road that led from the county highway to Brenna's residence. The journey on Whispering Trail was actually quite noisy with gravel grinding beneath the tires and clinking against the car's undercarriage; the road was named more for the secluded destination at the end. Her home was surrounded by deserted farm land once owned by her great, great grandparents. They shared the property. Her father and stepmother still lived in the old farmhouse where she grew up. She and Seth bought a double wide trailer when they got married and moved in next door. Three years later, when their daughter Libby was born, they extended the electrical lines to the far back corner of the property away from Seth's in-laws. Brenna bragged more than once to London that her husband's job as an electrician and resulting professional connections had saved their marriage.

Daylight was fading as the girls arrived at Brenna's house. Seth was in the front room watching television. Libby was at the kitchen table reading. This was London's first time meeting her friend's family. They had met 10 years earlier through a mutual friend at church, but had only become close since working together at the diner. Brenna's mother had passed away earlier that year from breast cancer. Having been the primary caregiver during her mom's illness, she became a great source of comfort and advice for London with her Grammy. London was a great source of comfort for her too in return. They had little else in common, but they bonded.

"Seth! It's eight-thirty. She's supposed to be in bed."

Libby looked up from her book and responded quickly. "Daddy said I could stay up until nine o'clock because I'm nine. Tyler's only four, so he had to go to bed. But I get to stay up. Right daddy? For 27 more minutes."

Seth smiled at his wife and shrugged. "That's right, Libby."

"You promised. Right daddy?"

"Yes, angel. I promised."

Brenna was clearly miffed at her husband's irresponsible behavior, but she didn't say anything more. Instead she gestured for Libby to come meet London. "This is my friend from work. Her name is London. Why don't you come say hi?"

Libby bounded from the kitchen chair and greeted London with an overzealous embrace. She didn't usually enjoy children, but she reciprocated Libby's hug to avoid hurting her feelings. Fortunately, the little girl was quickly distracted by Vienna sitting obediently by London's side.

"Hi doggy," Libby squeaked. "Do you want a huggy too?"

London could feel Vienna's happy tail tapping against her leg as she wagged excitedly. "You can hug her. She's a friendly dog."

"My kids are very affectionate. They love giving hugs," Brenna said.

Seth rose from his seat on the couch and greeted London too, introducing himself and shaking her hand. "They get the hugging thing from their mother. I'm more of a handshake kind of guy."

London cracked a smile, but despair and worry still tugged at the corners of her mouth. "I hope you don't mind Brenna dragging me home with her. Things are a little stressful at my place right now."

"You can stay as long as you need to," Seth replied. "Brenna told me about your grandma. I'm really sorry for your loss." Seth lacked the tough, rugged appearance London pictured in her mind, but he seemed as kind and generous as Brenna described.

"Thank you."

Brenna squeezed her husband's hand then tugged lightly on Libby's pony tail. "Do you and Daddy want to take London's doggy for a little walk before bedtime?"

"Oh Daddy. Can we? Can we?"

Seth smiled. Apparently he couldn't refuse his daughter's exuberant plea. Without a word, he took the leash from London's hand and started leading the dog out the front door. Libby skipped away behind them singing "London bridges falling down, falling down, falling down." London cringed.

London hated that song, remembering the bullying and ridiculing she endured as a child because of her name. When she was in second grade a group of boys, including Denny Chapman who was her friend at the time, formed a circle around her singing that song. They knocked her down on the playground blacktop and stole her Back to the Future lunch box. She was obsessed with that movie, convinced she could travel back in time to keep her mom from dying in that car accident. She never saw the lunch box ever again. And she never forgave Denny.

Brenna pointed down the hallway and encouraged London to follow. "Come on. I'll show you where you'll be staying."

The master bedroom and bath were located at one end of the trailer beyond the kitchen. At the opposite end was a second master-size bedroom. There was another bedroom and bathroom off the hallway in between. With help from Brenna's stepfather, Seth had built a wall to split the second large bedroom into separate rooms for the two kids. His mother, Colleen, practically moved in with Brenna and the kids whenever Seth travelled for work; she needed her own space. That's where London was sleeping during her visit.

"This is good ole Colleen's bedroom. That is until I can talk Seth into getting that woman her own trailer up by my dad's place." Brenna laughed. "I can't stand that woman."

London nudged past her through the doorway and into the bedroom. The room was small with mirrored closet doors that took up one entire wall.

"Aren't those doors tacky," Brenna commented. "Colleen's idea to make the room seem bigger. I think she just likes looking at herself."

London stared at her reflection, noting the large red welt on her right arm.

"Sorry. I guess I shouldn't talk about my husband's mom that way."

"Oh, I wasn't ignoring you," London said. "I was just noticing this spot on my arm."

"I saw that earlier. What happened?"

"A bee sting I guess," London said, gently rubbing her hand across the swollen skin. "I kind of remember dreaming about being stung. Maybe it wasn't a dream."

"Look. There's another one on your thigh." Brenna pressed against London's right side to turn her slightly toward the mirror so she could see it. "It looks like you got a little bruise too."

"Weird. I guess I'm allergic , but that's never happened before."

"Baking soda is supposed to help," Brenna suggested.

"No. It doesn't really sting. It's just a little sensitive to the touch. I'll be fine."

Seth entered the room behind Vienna and placed her leash on the end of the bed. "What are you girls talking about?"

"That spot on London's arm."

"That's a doozy," he said. "Did you have to get a shot at the doctor or something?"

"Now that you mention it, that is what it looks like. Little Tyler gets welts like that too when he gets shots."

"I didn't get any shots though," London said. She and Brenna froze staring at each other as though abruptly reaching the same conclusion. "No way."

"She wouldn't," Brenna said.

"No. She wouldn't do that," London said.

Seth threw his hands in the air. "Who wouldn't do what? What the hell are you two talking about?"

"Geneva!" Brenna exclaimed.

"You don't think she would drug me. Why would she do that?"

Brenna pulled her hands to her mouth and gasped. "Oh my God."

"No way," London said, taking a seat on the bed.

Vienna jumped onto the bed beside her momma. She started trying to lick her face, letting London know that her panic was making the dog nervous too.

"No way. She's a bitch but she isn't crazy. No way. No way."

"Why would somebody drug you?" Seth asked.

"That could explain why you didn't answer the phone or the door when I came over today. Or why you can't remember anything," Brenna suggested.

London tried harder to remember exactly what happened at Grammy's memorial service. Still, she couldn't recall anything about that day after making her second screwdriver. "Did you see me drinking at Grammy's service?"

"I saw you with a drink. I assumed it was something stronger than plain orange juice, but I didn't know for sure. And I didn't ask. You didn't seem drunk though when I left."

"I don't even remember seeing you leave," London said. "Were there a lot of people still there?"

"No, I was one of the last. I left right behind Calvin and Collette."

"Did Calvin say anything about work today? When I didn't show up, do you think he knew I was drunk?"

Brenna kneeled on the bed next to London and grabbed her shoulders to calm her. "You're spinning now. Calm down. You weren't acting like a drunk person. I promise. I wouldn't lie to you about that."

"So things must have gone downhill after you left." London paused, still reeling from the possibility that Geneva might have injected her with something. "Were Geneva and Alma-Rae still there?"

"No, they were gone too."

Seth stepped further into the room. "London, I don't like what I'm hearing here. I'm going to call Harrison down at the sheriff's office and have him come..."

"No. Please no. This is crazy," London insisted. "Why would she drug me? I could see her trying to kill me for the estate money, but there's no way she'd do it on the day of Grammy's service. She's an idiot, but I'd like to think she's at least smart enough to know that the cops would immediately suspect her. I think I'm just being paranoid."

"These past few weeks have been pretty stressful," Brenna conceded.

"Maybe we should let you get some sleep," Seth said, moving her bags from the foot of the bed over to the corner of the room.

"That's a good idea, Seth." Brenna rose from the edge of the bed and wrapped her arm around her husband's back. "We'll go so that you can rest, London. It's after nine o'clock. I need to get Miss Libby into bed anyway."

"I have to call Calvin and explain why I didn't show up today."

"It's too late to call now," Brenna said. "I'm working the early shift with him tomorrow. I'll let him know you're okay and that you just need a few more days. I know he'll understand."

London thanked them and said goodnight. She was feeling slightly guilty for making such an outrageous accusation about someone her grandmother trusted. Grammy was a trusting person by nature, but she also had a knack for knowing when something was awry. Geneva was manipulative, but Grammy's instincts were sharp. Certainly she would have known if Geneva was capable of something so hateful and destructive.

For the first time in years, London started thinking about her high school classmate Allyssa Roubideaux. They were best friends, notoriously getting into trouble together. Grammy always discouraged them spending time together, but couldn't choose London's friends for her... not when she was 19 years old. London remembered vividly the night she got caught sneaking into the house after drinking purple passion at Allyssa's birthday party. She couldn't remember the punishment, though it was harsh, but she remembered the guilt and shame. She felt the same again as she imagined Grammy looking down at her from heaven and hearing the hateful, awful things she was saying about her own sister. Grammy and Grampy always set a good example for their granddaughter in terms of forgiveness, respect, and charity. London was admittedly a slow learner. Respecting Geneva was one thing. Running home with her tail between her legs was out of the question.

Chapter Five

Most of Coral Leaf's residential areas were remote, secluded spaces tucked away in the shadows of tall, majestic mountains. Brenna's family property was no different. Her backyard was Affinity Peak, better known as "Ghost Mountain". Legends and old wives' tales spoke of mystery and unexplained tragedies, but the name was really derived from the towering trees and lush greenery that made it impossible to determine where the tree trunks sprouted from the hillside. London studied Ghost Mountain for a fourth grade English project, but this was the closest she'd ever been. The view reminded her of the beauty she once saw in her own backyard, before greed destroyed Mount Karma's majesty. She'd never before wished for her mother's painting talent, but she desperately wanted that view to take home with her. A snapshot with her camera phone just wasn't good enough.

London noticed as she returned her phone to her back pocket that she had no signal. That wasn't unusual; there were still many places in Coral Leaf, including Grammy's place, where cell service was unavailable. She felt different about it this time, slightly more cut off from the world. Brenna and Seth were both at work and the kids were at daycare. The farmhouse where Brenna's father lived was almost two miles away and he was their nearest neighbor. She wasn't afraid necessarily, but being there alone all day without her car was a little creepy. Perhaps the legends of Ghost Mountain had seeped into her subconscious.

Reading was always a great distraction for London when she was scared or lonely. After her creepy morning adventure hike, she liked the idea of spending the afternoon sitting pool side with a book. Although in this case, that meant sitting in a wobbly lawn chair with her feet in a plastic kiddy pool. At least she had good odds of finding something worth reading. Brenna had three book shelves in her living room and a small library of romance novels for her to choose from. She picked one titled *Built for Love* with a sexy, rugged-looking construction worker on the front cover. This choice was ironic given her appreciation for the lack of construction traffic and noise at home. Brenna definitely teased her about that when she got home from work that afternoon.

"I knew you had a thing for Baxter. I just knew it."

"What are you talking about?"

"Built for Love? Grow out his hair and smack on a nappy beard and that guy on the cover looks just like him," Brenna teased.

London pulled her feet from the pool as Tyler started splashing the water with his hands. "It's your book. Maybe you're the one who has the hots for him." She laughed and gestured for Tyler to splash in the other direction towards Brenna. "You should splash your mommy, Tyler."

"No no. Tyler, don't you splash mommy." Brenna scooped her son up in her arms, pointed her finger at London, and began scolding her with baby talk. "You tell London she isn't being nice. Huh?"

Tyler grinned bashfully and buried his face in his mother's shoulder.

"He's my shy little guy," Brenna said.

London smiled.

"Why don't we go inside? It's so hot and humid out here I can barely breathe." Brenna motioned for London to follow her inside. "I promised Tyler he could watch cartoons while Libby is at swimming lessons. You can help me make tacos for dinner. And we can talk more about your cute little crush."

London kneeled down to pet Vienna as the dog greeted them at the door. She ignored the comment about her crush. "I was wondering where Libby was."

"Swimming class three days a week. I pick her up at daycare then drop her off at her friend's Lucy's house. Lucy's mom takes them to the community center. Seth stops by when he gets off work then brings her home," Brenna explained. "It's a highly coordinated effort. But I think that little bit of independence has helped. Libby used to be really shy too like this little guy."

Brenna kissed Tyler on the forehead, handed him the sippy cup, and put him down so he could go watch his cartoons. The little boy swerved to his left as far as possible to avoid London, then passed by her without making eye contact.

"I think he's scared of me."

"He's always that way around people he doesn't know. Libby grew out of it. He probably will too."

"I can't believe Libby was ever that shy," London said.

"Seth and I used to have to take turns holding her anytime we went anywhere. Now she'll talk to anybody. I worry sometimes that she's too friendly to everybody. Seth and I are constantly having to remind her that you don't talk to strangers."

London nodded.

"But anyway, I want to talk more about why you were reading that book."

"I don't know why you're making such a big deal about it. It's just the first one I grabbed," London lied.

"You are such a liar. It's a good thing we came inside. Otherwise God might strike you down with lightening," Brenna teased. "Your face is bright red. And you have that goofy grin on your face like when he flirts with you at the diner."

"I do not got a goofy grin on..."

"Yes you do," Brenna interrupted. "Why won't you admit that you like him?"

London contemplated for a few seconds before answering. She wasn't afraid of admitting the truth to Brenna. She was afraid of admitting the truth to herself. "I can't be with someone who works for the Wickerfords. Geneva says people already think I was in on Brody's scams. Me and Baxter together would be quite the scandal."

Brenna stared at London. Her facial expression reflected both surprise and sympathy.

"Don't look at me that way, Brenna."

"I can't believe you're letting Geneva get to you. Nobody who knows you... Nobody who *really* knows you would ever think that. I don't think it's possible for anyone to love another person more than you loved your Grammy. People see that. Baxter sees that too I'm sure. That's probably why he's so crazy about you."

"I don't know about that."

Brenna grabbed London's shoulders and stared intently in her face. "Geneva is the one who swooped into town on her broomstick at the last minute. She had 27 years to find your grandmother and never bothered until now. And need I remind you that she's the one practically living with Alma-Rae?"

"That's a good point I guess."

"Plus I still swear she injected you with something."

"That was just some stupid theory. I was drunk. There were empty bottles of booze all over my bedroom. She wouldn't have drugged me." London grabbed a glass from the cupboard and poured herself some lemonade. "I wish I hadn't said anything about that."

"Okay, but still nobody is going to care if you're dating someone who works for the Wickerfords. Hell, that family signs almost half the paychecks in this town anyway."

"I still need to think about it some more."

Brenna walked about the kitchen collecting items from the refrigerator and pantry. "Well I wouldn't worry about what Geneva says. Nobody is going to care. So if you like him..."

"I didn't say that," London interrupted.

"Okay, so when you're finally willing to admit that you like him, you should go out with him. Just one date."

London rolled her eyes and chuckled. "We'll see."

"I know he misses you at the diner. Everybody does. He asked about you yesterday wondering when you were coming back. He seemed bummed when I said you were taking the rest of the week."

"I think I'm going back to work tomorrow," London said.

"Really?"

"It's just a little too quiet around here during the day. I got a little spooked today."

Brenna opened the Tupperware container she'd retrieved from the refrigerator and poured some pre-cooked ground beef into a skillet on the stove. Then she joined London at the kitchen table. "What do you mean spooked?"

"It's kind of hard to describe," London said, helping Brenna arrange taco shells onto a cookie sheet. "Almost like that feeling you get when there's a bad storm coming. Just a real eerie, uneasy feeling. Like something bad was going to happen."

"I hate that feeling."

"I know. Right? And I felt totally helpless without my car. My cell phone doesn't work out here either."

"Oh, sorry. I'm so used to that, I didn't even think to mention it. Our home phone works though."

"I'm used to it too. I don't hardly get service at my house either, but for some reason it really bothered me today. I can't explain it."

"London, your whole world has been turned upside down in this past week. That eerie feeling is probably just uncertainty about your future. You've gotta figure out now what you're going to do next."

"I'm not ready to think about my future without Grammy. Not yet."

"You don't have to, sweetie. Just take it one day at a time," Brenna said, rising from her chair to check the stove. "After dinner I'll take you by your house to get your car. That way maybe you won't feel so isolated."

"I'm still going back to work tomorrow though."

"Okay sure. I'm not going to argue with you on that. You're staying here though. Right? For a few more days? I think you need a break from Geneva and her bologna."

London chuckled. "Bologna?"

"You know what I mean." Brenna glanced over toward the couch at her little boy watching cartoons. "I don't cuss in front of the kids."

London got up from the table and brought the tray of taco shells for Brenna to put into the oven. She didn't give Brenna a definite answer about staying, but she agreed that she needed a break from Geneva. She thought if she could get past the creepy feeling, she would probably stay out there forever. Whispering Trail would be the perfect hideout for her when she finally lost her mind and killed Geneva. Or better yet, the perfect spot to bury the body. Brenna's family had more than 100 acres; nobody would even know she was there. Then she realized those thoughts were exactly why she needed a break from Geneva.

Lake Amethyst was the largest lake in West Virginia and was bordered by three towns: Coral Leaf, Connors Bluff, and Kenrickson Cove. The Fourth of July fireworks were launched every year from a marina in Kenrickson Cove, right where the water curved around behind Mount Karma. London found out when she returned to work on Thursday that the Kenrickson Cove Patriot's Festival, as they called it, was also hosting a fireworks display on July third. She was so pleased. Before Grammy got sick London used to take her out in the boat to watch the shows, just like Grampy did when he was alive. Even after losing her sight, Grammy loved hearing the loud booms. She hoped heaven had restored Grammy's eye sight and that she'd finally get to enjoy the bright, beautiful colors once again, this time with her soul mate by her side and a magnificent, cloudless view from above.

Calvin always closed the diner and set up a vending station during the Patriot's Festival. London and Brenna both had the day off on Saturday; they decided to attend at the festival together. Seth quickly disappeared in search of the beer garden. Brenna and London spent the day taking Tyler and Libby around to the various carnival rides and games booths. Almost everyone they knew went annually for the event, but with over 3,000 people from the various townships London and Brenna were at times lost amidst a crowd of strangers. Although many of those strangers knew Vera and Montgomery Keller. London was stopped many times throughout the day by people wanting to offer their condolences. She was touched and honored that her grandparents were so loved by the community.

Despite an initial desire to skip the daytime festivities London enjoyed a wonderful afternoon with her best friend, at least until too much sun and cotton candy spoiled Libby's tummy and everyone else's fun. The little girl told her mom she didn't feel well, then abruptly threw up all over her favorite sundress. Brenna took off with the kids to the bathrooms; London headed to the beer garden to find Seth.

The girls had purposely avoided the beer garden all day. First of all, a tent full of drunk people was not an ideal environment for children. Second of all, they predicted Geneva would be there with Alma-Rae and her rich bitch society women, Charlynn Madison and Janice Elgin. Charlynn married into wealth three times, then divorced three times into even more wealth. Like Alma-Rae, Janice was born into a rich family. She was technically still married to her husband Vincent, but she hadn't seen him in over 2 years. He was living in Italy trying to be an artist on her dime. Everyone knew the three women secretly hated each other and they loved to compete for the hot, young construction workers — buying sexual favors with the false promise of striking gold. London had seen them do it dozens of times.

Geneva was the first person London spotted as she entered the beer garden tent. As predicted, she was right in the middle of Alma-Rae's circle and she was clearly a threat to the other members of that society. Even Alma-Rae seemed annoyed by the attention the younger, prettier soon-to-be-millionaire was receiving from her usual handsome prey. London realized that perhaps she had misjudged that relationship. From the beginning she believed Geneva was using Alma-Rae, but suddenly she questioned if it was the other way around. Those two deserved each other too.

A voice called out to London from behind as she continued moving through the tent in search of Brenna's husband. "London. I was hoping I'd see you here today."

She immediately recognized the voice and spun around to face him. "Hadley. Hi."

He leaned in and hugged her, and spoke softly into her ear. "I was really sorry to hear about your grandma. I know she was really special to you."

"Thanks. And yes, she was very, very special to me. I miss her so much."

"I wanted to come pay my respects at the funeral, but I was in Florida with my sister and her family. I didn't know 'til I got home that she passed. I'm really sorry, London."

"It's okay, Hadley. Thank you," London said, gently squeezing his shoulder. "How is Leila? I haven't seen her since high school."

"She's good. She's got two little girls now and her husband got his self a good job too. Leila says maybe I should come down there and live with them. But I got me a girlfriend now."

"Anybody I know?"

"Her name is Alexis. I don't think you know her. She's from Nebraska, but is living here now with her brother and his family. She works with the horses down at my cousin Burke's place. She's really pretty and super nice. I know you'd like her, London."

London smiled. "I hope I get to meet her some time. It's really good to see you so happy, Hadley. I know things were hard for you after Macey."

"We broke up over five years ago. I finally decided it was time to stop living in the past. It was time for me to move on."

"It's good to hear you say that too," London said, kissing him on the cheek. "I have to get a move on too. Have you seen Seth Reese, Brenna's husband? His little girl is sick. Brenna wants to take her home."

"I saw him earlier I think. He was talking to Baxter."

London wanted to press for more details, but she resisted. "Well this tent isn't that big. I should be able to find him. I'll talk to you later. Okay? You bring your girl by the house some time so I can meet her."

"Okay. That sounds like a plan."

London smiled at Hadley then started pushing her way through the crowd forming to listen to the live music starting at seven o'clock. She walked the perimeter of the space twice, but still couldn't find him. Brenna was surely wondering what was taking so long; she was surprised her friend hadn't come looking for her husband at that point too. Then she spotted him exiting one of the porta-johns just outside the side tent entrance. She quickly alerted him to the situation with Libby and started him leading back to where Brenna awaited. Libby's upset stomach had spoiled the family's plan to join London later that evening for fireworks. London was on her own.

Chapter Six

Vienna, like most dogs, was afraid of fireworks, so London left the dog behind out the house when she headed out that evening to watch the show on Grampy's boat. Unfortunately when she returned to the house, the back screen door was swinging open and her dog was nowhere in sight. Her initial reaction was not to panic. The loud explosions were scary; Vienna was probably hiding under one of the beds. No. In Grammy's closet? No. Behind the couch? No. In the laundry room? No. Under the beds? Still no. London was starting to panic and was fearing the worst. London forgot to latch the screen door when she left and Vienna had run away. Her dog, her best friend, and her only family was gone forever. Those were the thoughts suddenly racing through London's frantic mind as she dashed around in the darkness with a flashlight, calling out Vienna's name. She was gone.

London traced her steps back to the boat house still calling out the dog's name. She heard nothing in response except chirping tree frogs and the sound of waves lapping against hard surfaces that disrupted their natural ripple toward the lake shore. She continued into the woods that occupied the back 20 acres of her grandmother's property, using the moon as her guide after the batteries in her flashlight died. She knew the landscape well enough. She had tracked through those woods many times, though never through the dark as she did on this night. She feared not for her own safety, but for Vienna's welfare out in the wilderness all by herself.

Adrenaline kept London wandering until first morning light, completely unphased by the twigs and broken branches scraping against her ankles as she passed. All hope was gone after searching all night, but she pressed on until the summer heat and dehydration made it impossible for her to continue. She cursed toward the heavens for mercy. "Please give me my dog back. Please! Please!"

The heavens did not reply.

Every tear London held back during her grandmother's illness and death trailed readily from her eyes as her legs crumpled beneath her. She collapsed at the base of a giant oak tree and against its thick, twisted roots that long ago outgrew the depths of the surrounding soil. There was no hope at this point. Vienna was a poor, defenseless wiener dog. There were wild animals in the area probably capable of swallowing her whole. London felt like her life was over. And she would have given her life to go back in time and latch that stupid screen door. Maybe death was too good for her. She deserved the hell she had created for herself.

London returned to her house, defeated and drained of all emotion. She drenched her hair beneath the garden hose, soaked a dish towel in the kitchen sink and wrapped it around the back of her neck. She retrieved a bottle of her Grammy's favorite orange soda from the refrigerator then hopped onto the counter. She sipped slowly to avoid getting sick.

"This has to be a nightmare," she said to herself. She glanced down at the bloody scratches and wounds on her legs and feet, no longer oblivious to the painful sting. Her cheap rubber flip flops were caked with mud, her shorts were torn, and her tank top was soaking wet from the garden hose. This was no time for company, but there was a knock at the door.

Her visitor knocked a second time before London reached the door, though she walked quickly in hopes that someone had found her beloved pet. She called out Vienna's name as she opened the door.

"No. It's Baxter."

He chuckled, but his attempt at humor was met with inconsolable crying.

"Hey. Hey. What's the matter?"

London turned away with her face buried in her hands.

"London. What is it, honey? Are you okay?"

"No!" she screamed. "I am not okay. My dog is..." She couldn't bear to finish the sentence.

"What about your dog?"

"She's gone. Vienna is gone."

Baxter hooked his meaty arms around her and pulled her body close to his. "She's gone? What do you mean, honey?"

"She ran away. And I ..."

"We'll find her." Baxter kissed her brow softly and tightened his embrace. "I'll help you."

"No. It's no use. She's gone. And it's all my fault."

London sobbed uncontrollably, clinging helplessly to him. Baxter spoke softly in her ear. She was crying too hard to hear most of what he was saying, so his words offered little comfort. His embrace, on the other hand, was a welcomed gesture. She lingered there, thankful for an escape from the solitude she felt. The strength of his arms made her feel secure and made her forget the reasons she had rejected him all those times before. Through tears and desperation she kissed him, softly at first then once again with more passion... And more tongue. His kiss tasted sweet like the tea she served him every day at the diner. His callused hands felt like sandpaper against her soft, pampered skin, but she liked it.

Baxter had been staring at her chest since he arrived, admiring the way her nipples shone through the wet tank top clinging tightly around the curves of her breasts. She knew he wanted her. He made no protest as she led him through the kitchen and down the hall to her bedroom. He said nothing as she peeled the sticky clothing from her body. He was Pavlov's dog and she just rang his bell.

Every muscle flexed and bulged as he unbuttoned his shirt, almost as though strategically choreographed for her pleasure.

His eyes were alight, burning hot like the flame-engulfed dragon tattooed on his chest. She no longer had control of her actions. She had no understanding of her behavior. This wasn't love. This was dirty, uninhibited carnal desire. Her mouth watered and her body tensed as she felt his weight shift the bed beneath her. Ice cubes clinked against the glass as Baxter plucked one from the water glass on her bedside table. He traced the ice down her neck and circled her hardening nipples, alternating from side to side between the frigid ice and the heated cavern of his mouth. She closed her eyes and plunged deeper into a whirling sea of lust and passion. The weight of his body overwhelmed her as he moved into position between her thighs. The heat of his breath on her flesh felt like... Wait. London couldn't finish that thought.

Something wasn't right. Her beloved dog was lost. She'd been out all night in the woods looking for him. There was no glass on her bedside table. There were no ice cubes. She opened her eyes to the disappointing view of her black and white checkered kitchen floor and the reality of the latest tragedy unfolding in her life. Vienna *was* gone. She was all alone.

London hopped down from the kitchen counter. She was overwhelmed by shame and feeling like the most selfish, despicable human being on the planet. How could she rest not knowing what happened to her poor, defenseless dog? How could she daydream about such disgusting behavior with that grungy neanderthal? Grammy had only been gone for two weeks and the dog she loved – the dog London vowed to take care of – was lost and alone somewhere. She grabbed a shirt blindly from the top of the clean clothes basket as she passed through the laundry room, then ventured out the back door.

The late afternoon sun followed London as she moved slowly toward the western edge of the property. The sun-scorched earth burned London's feet through the thin rubber soles of her sandals. She felt the pain, but kept walking, headed straight for the Wickerford's mansion atop the steep hillside. Her latest theory or conclusion was that Geneva had stolen Vienna. She had traced every step of every acre and found no trace of the little pooch. The thought occurred to London that an animal had carried her away. The animal named Geneva came to mind immediately.

Geneva, apparently spotting London from one of the front windows, greeted her angry sister at the front porch. "You been on another drinkin' binge? You look like shit."

"Where is my dog? I know you took her."

"I don't have your dog."

London pressed forward with angry, deliberate steps. "I said where is my dog?"

"And I said I don't have your skanky dog." Geneva's reply was hostile, as were her movements down the front stairs.

"Give me my fucking dog!" London screamed, charging a few more steps forward.

"Give me my fucking shirt! You're stinking it up and stretching it all out with those gi-normous boobs of yours."

London stripped the shirt from her back and threw it at her. "Jealous?"

"Hardly," Geneva grunted. She held up the red tee shirt and pointed to the fiery dragon screen-print on the chest. "This is just my favorite shirt. My friend Derrick plays guitar in this band. Dragon Crush. He gave this to me the last time I saw him."

London stared at the shirt, stunned at first by the dragon's resemblance to the tattoo she imagined on Baxter's chest. She hadn't noticed the design as she grabbed it on her way out the door, but she must have seen it on top of the laundry basket. She had never even seen Baxter without his shirt on, but that seemed a strange coincidence just the same.

"These guys are gonna' be famous some day. I just know it," Geneva continued.

"Look, I don't care about your stupid shirt or your stupid friend Derrick. I just want my fucking dog back."

London took another step up then shoved Geneva. She fell backward, landing hard on her ass and scraping the back of her legs on the rough stone finish.

"Give! Me! My! Fucking! Dog! Back!" she screamed.

Alma-Rae heard the commotion from inside and came to the front door just as London stomped on Geneva's hand. "What the hell is going on here?"

London stepped back as Alma-Rae approached and started helping Geneva get up.

"Are you okay, Evie?"

"I'm fine," she whimpered, massaging her hand dramatically. "London is accusing me of taking her dog."

"You did take her! I know you did."

"London, why would she take your dog?" Alma-Rae's tone hinged on condescending and disbelief.

"Because that's the kind of person she is, Alma-Rae. She's a cold-hearted bitch."

Geneva flipped her the bird.

"That kind of talk is uncalled for. Your sister has been nothing' but nice to you since she got here and all you've tried to do is run her out of town."

"Is your dog even missing, London? Or are you just making that up to make me look bad?"

"You stole her. I know you stole her. You took her while I was at the fireworks last night." London was emotionally and physically exhausted at this point. All her fight was gone. She crumbled into tears on Alma-Rae's front steps. "Please, just give me my dog back."

"I told you! I didn't take your..."

Alma-Rae interrupted Geneva's sentence and motioned for her to go into the house. "You go inside. I'll handle this."

"But I didn't..."

"I know you didn't. Just let me talk to her."

London was in no mood for a pep talk, but she sensed by Alma-Rae's tone that was about to happen. Unfortunately, she was entirely too defeated to run. If Geneva really hadn't taken Vienna then London knew she would probably never find her again.

"Honey, I know you've been having a hard time since your grandmother died and all. Evie told me all about the drinkin' and everything. And I feel really bad for you. But she didn't take your dog. She couldn't have. She's been with me the whole time."

All hope was crushed.

"I know we ain't been close in a lot of years, but I always liked your grandma. Me and your mom and my brother Harlan were really close when we were kids. Our mom and dad were always busy working and making money and traveling. Your grandma was really good to us. She even taught me how to cook and crochet."

London sniffled. She couldn't believe Alma-Rae was being so kind. "What happened? Why were Grammy and Wick so mad at each other?"

"Nobody knows," she replied. "There are lots of rumors and theories out there, but my dad wouldn't tell us."

"Grammy wouldn't tell me either."

Alma-Rae sat down on the step next to London. "I guess it doesn't really matter. I just wanted you to know that I'm really sorry about her passing. And I'm sorry about the dog too."

"Grammy loved that dog so much."

"Maybe they were just meant to stay together," Alma-Rae suggested. "I believe in that kind of stuff."

London shrugged her shoulders. She made no comment on the subject. Instead she thanked Alma-Rae for her kindness and started down the steps. She turned as reached the edge of the driveway and called out. "Tell Geneva I'm sorry."

"Okay. You take care, London."

Alma-Rae's insight didn't necessarily make London feel better, but she believed in that kind of stuff. Grammy definitely loved Vienna enough to warrant heavenly intervention to reunite the pair. London was with her the day she adopted Vienna and she truly believed it was love at first sight for both of them. She remembered vividly the look on her grandmother's face when that sweet little dog peered at her through the wire cage door. She was clearly frightened, but trusting enough to let Grammy pet her.

The Keller family always had a dog except for the first two years after Grampy's big coon hound Woodrow passed away. Woodrow was a gigantic lap dog. He loved people and he loved attention. He also loved steeling food from the edge of the counter when nobody was looking. Grammy complained about cleaning up slobber, dog hair, and muddy paw prints, but she was truly heartbroken when she had to say goodbye to the loveable fellow. His death left a void in her heart that no other dog could fill. Then along came a happy, yappy little wiener dog named Sally May, who was later renamed Vienna because she looked like a little sausage. London long believed fate had guided them to that adoption event that day. Maybe Alma-Rae was right, but that possibility didn't make London feel any less guilty for leaving the screen door open.

As she neared the bottom of the hill on her way back home, London spotted Baxter's vintage pickup truck in her driveway. She couldn't see his face, he'd parked the truck at too much of an angle, but the vehicle was unmistakably his. There wasn't another person in town with an old beat up, orange and white GMC pickup. He had been trying to get a date with her for months and had passed by the house every day on his way to work, but he had never before showed up at her door. A visit from him at this point seemed like another very strange coincidence. Baxter hopped out of his truck as she approached. He looked very happy to see her. She was in no mood for any more strange coincidences.

"What are you doing here?" she shouted.

"That's the nice thing about living out here in the middle of nowhere. You can shout as loud as you want and nobody's around to get upset with you."

"I'm not shouting. I'm just..."

London halted her words as Baxter stopped in front of her. He was smiling broadly. Thanks to her earlier daydream, she was unusually self-conscious about her breasts. Her tank top was mostly dry by this time, but he was standing especially close. She folded her arms tightly against her chest just in case.

"Come here," he said, looping his arm around her back and leading her toward the house.

"Are you drunk or something?"

"I'm not drunk. I'm just happy."

She steered away from him, but he grabbed her again as they neared the pickup. "I have a surprise for you."

" I'm not going anywhere with you." London took a step back and pulled away from him again.

"In about 10 seconds you are going to feel really bad for doubting me."

Baxter smiled and started squeezing the push-button door handle. That's when she heard the most beautiful sound. Like music to her ears, London heard Vienna's distinct bark and it was coming from inside the cab of his truck. Suddenly, Vienna's furry little head appeared in the window. Baxter was right. She felt really bad.

"Oh my God, Vienna!" she exclaimed, rushing to retrieve her as he pulled the door open. Vienna practically leaped into her arms, wagging her tail and smothering London's face with kisses. Tears of joy and relief blurred her eyes. "You found my dog? I can't believe you found my dog! Oh my God, I thought she was gone forever."

"I was on my way to drop off some blueprints at the construction site and saw her roaming over there in that field."

"I'm so glad to have you home, Vienna!" London snuggled the dog tightly against her chest and repeatedly kissed the top of her head. "Oh, Baxter! How can I ever thank you?"

"You don't have to thank me. I'm just happy I was able to bring her home."

"Okay, well how about a tall glass of lemonade? Or some sweet tea? You're a hero. I've gotta' do something for you."

A cheerful smile sparkled in his pale blue eyes. "It's okay. You really don't have to thank me, London. I'd hope most people would do the same around here."

"I would hope so too, but I'm still extremely thankful."

London leaned in and kissed Baxter on the cheek. He smiled then got back into his truck to leave. He said nothing more; he just waved goodbye as he backed down the driveway. She was somewhat surprised he turned down the opportunity to come inside or that he hadn't used her gratitude as leverage to convince her to go out with him. Perhaps that was part of his plan to make her want him more. If so, the plan was working.

Chapter Seven

Chocolate pudding was London's all-time favorite dessert. While most other families congregated at Penguin Pete's Frozen Custard place for half-off independence day concretes, Grammy, Grampy, and London always returned home after the fireworks display and made chocolate pudding parfaits with whipped cream and chocolate shavings on top. London was too nervous to leave Vienna again for the fireworks on July Fourth, so she decided to celebrate her memories and pay tribute to her grandparents with chocolate pudding... And not the kind from the plastic cups always stocked in her refrigerator. There was something magical about making it with the cocoa, sugar, and milk like Grammy always did. She hadn't enjoyed that tradition in over 20 years.

There were many traditions London enjoyed with her grandparents. She never took their love and attention for granted, even as a teenager. She knew she was lucky. She also knew that somewhere in the world there was another little girl whom they'd given up when her mother died. That little girl was raised by strangers and judging from the way she'd been acting since her arrival, those strangers had not cared for her the way Grammy and Grampy would have cared for her. Alma-Rae's words had gotten to London. She wished she'd been more welcoming when her baby sister finally came home.

London revealed this epiphany to Brenna when they worked together on Monday morning. Their work shift started an hour earlier that day to handle extra setup from being closed the whole weekend. Collette was in the kitchen baking some cookies and fresh pies; Brenna and London were in the dining room alone together.

"Now you feel sorry for her?" Brenna challenged, replacing the lids on the salt shakers she just filled. "You're starting to sound like Dr. Jeckyl and Mr. Hyde."

"I pushed her. I knocked her down," London grunted. "I don't care what she's said to me, she didn't deserve that. I mean what kind of person does that to their own sister?"

Brenna chuckled.

"It's not funny."

"London, you are one of the nicest people I know. She pushes your buttons. I don't know why, but you wouldn't just hate on her for no reason."

"Like what?"

Brenna moved from her makeshift work station at the counter and sat down at the table across from where London was wrapping the silverware. She grabbed the napkin from London's hand. "She's rude and crude. And she certainly isn't trustworthy. Seriously, any woman willing to sleep with Denny Chapman has some serious judgment issues."

They both laughed.

"In her defense though..."

"In her defense?" Brenna gasped. "I'm going to stop you right there. You are not going to defend that tramp. No way. Ain't happening!"

London laughed. "Stop it."

"No. You stop it."

London took the napkin back from Brenna and continued with her work. "I have to stop hating her so much. I was so mad at her yesterday I could have... well, I don't even want to finish what I was going to say. But it wasn't good. It was a little scary."

"I get it," Brenna said, returning to the counter. "It's not good to let yourself get that upset. But in *your* defense, you thought she had stolen your dog."

"Yea, but she didn't," London argued. "I can't tell you how thankful I was when I saw her cute little face pop up and stare at me through the window."

"She's such a sweet pup."

"I went straight to bed after Baxter left. She was right beside me, curled up in the small of my back like she always does. I don't know what I would have done if he hadn't found her."

"Good thing he realized she was yours." Brenna wiped down the final panel of glass on the bakery display case then joined London at the table again to help with a second tray of napkin silverware roll-ups.

"She was wearing her tags," London replied. "Besides, it's only me and the Wickerfords down there in that little valley. And he knew I had a dog. We talked about it one time."

"Really?"

"He was talking about the dog he had when he lived in Kentucky."

"I thought he was from Arizona."

"I think he's moved around a lot," London said. "Anyway, he said he was on his way to the construction site and saw her wondering in the field. I swear I could have kissed him."

"You should have! He would have loved it."

Brenna's excitement seemed like the perfect segue into a discussion about her sexy daydream, but London decided to keep that a secret.

"Your face is as red as that tablecloth, London."

"Don't make fun of me now."

Brenna shook her head. "I am not making fun of you. I'm just kind of surprised it's taken you this long to admit you like him. He's been after you for months to go out with him."

"I didn't say I liked him. He rescued my dog."

"You can deny it all you want, but I know you like him. I wasn't sure about him at first. I thought he was too pushy, but now..."

"It doesn't matter now anyway. I gave him at least three chances yesterday to ask me out and he didn't. I think he's lost interest."

"Doubtful," Brenna said. "Look at you. You are gorgeous and sweet and kind and generous and..."

"Okay, stop."

"And incredibly humble." Brenna stuck her tongue out and laughed.

"Trust me. He hasn't asked me out in a long time. The guy has moved on."

"We'll see," Brenna insisted.

London said nothing more on the subject, but she recognized the increased difficulty she was having denying her feelings. The daydream likely had more to do with helplessness than with sex — she remembered reading that in one of her psychology books one time — but there was little doubt that her attraction was growing. Brenna clearly saw the signs. London wondered how well she had hidden her secret from Baxter so far. Maybe she hid her feelings too well and maybe that was why he stopped asking her out. Maybe she blew it. She didn't know for sure. The only thing she knew for sure was that she desperately needed a distraction. The fates obliged a few hours later. In walked Brody Danbrook.

Brody was as handsome and charming as they come. He was the love of London's life, the man she planned to marry until greed ruined her happily-ever-after fairy tale fantasy. He strolled into the diner that morning and immediately caught the eye of every woman still lingering there at the end of the early breakfast rush. London was at one time defenseless to his charming ways; she learned that lesson the hard way and had since grown to pity those still victim to his act. At this point, watching him flash that smile to all the pretty ladies made her sick to her stomach.

London's eyes met Brenna's across the room. Neither said a word or made a single gesture. They both knew. He had just taken a seat in London's station, but she was not going to wait on him. London retreated quickly to the kitchen while Brenna made her way toward the selfish asshole. She watched and listened from the pick-up window.

"What do you want?" Brenna growled.

"I need to talk to London."

London caught his eye from her hiding spot, but she avoided eye contact.

"She's busy helping real customers. So you're stuck with me." Brenna retrieved her order note pad from the front pocket of her apron. She positioned herself between him and his view of London then continued. "Now what do you want to order, Mr. Hollywood? This table is for paying customers."

"I guess just bring me two eggs, sunny-side up, and a side of bacon."

"Whatever," she grunted. "You know I'm going to spit in your food. Right?"

Brody tugged lightly at her arm. "Look, I know what London told you, but you only heard one side of the story. I am not the bad guy."

"Oh shut up. I have work to do." Brenna mumbled a few obscenities then walked away without giving him a chance to say anything more. She poked her head into the kitchen. "Do you want me to kick him out of here?"

"No."

"You know I'll do it," Brenna bragged. Hope twinkled in her eye. "It would be my pleasure to do it."

"No. Don't make a scene. You know how Calvin feels about that." London arched her back and took a deep breath. "I can handle this. I'll just ignore him."

Ignoring Brody Danbrook was much easier said than done. A salesman by trade, he always knew the exact right things to say. Plus this was the first time she'd seen him in over a year. He disappeared from Coral Leaf right after they broke up and she never expected to see him again. The reason for his stop at the diner was no mystery; he obviously heard of Grammy's death and was hoping to cash in. London was not even going to let him get one foot in the door this time, even if part of her was curious about what he had to say.

London returned to the dining room with a tray of food. She pretended not to notice he was calling out to her as she passed by his table and engaged in casual conversation with her customers as though he wasn't even there.

"So Tracy, how is little Miss Sadie doing?" she asked.

"My husband is spoiling her rotten," Tracy replied, holding up her cell phone to display a picture of her adorable malshipoo puppy.

"She is so tiny and cute."

"Thanks. Don't let this sweet little face fool you. She is..."

Brody got up from his seat at the nearby table and interrupted London's conversation. "London, I need to talk to you."

London was embarrassed. Tracy was obviously stunned.

"I'm sorry, Tracy. Can you please excuse me?"

London led him away from Tracy's table, gritting her teeth and scolding him.

"That was incredibly rude. How dare you?"

"I didn't know any other way to get you to talk to me," he replied. He grabbed her shoulder as they reached the open area near the front doors and forced her to face him. "It's important."

Brody wasn't yelling or raising his voice, but the other customers were taking notice of their interaction.

"You are embarrassing me."

"Let's step outside then. Just for a minute."

Brenna was standing nearby, shaking her head frantically.

"No," London refused. "I know why you're here. Now that Grammy is gone you want me back. You're gonna' tell me how much you love me and how much you've missed me and blah blah blah. I'm not falling for it again, Brody."

Brody stepped back as though he was stunned by London's comment. "That's not why I'm here."

"Sure," she doubted.

"Seriously, London. I don't want to get back together. I'm with somebody else now and..." Brody paused and glanced around the room. People were staring. "Now come on, let's talk outside where we can have some privacy."

"London has work to do," Brenna interjected.

London held out her hand to hush her friend. "Like Brenna said, I am busy here Brody. Just say what you came to say then leave me alone."

He glanced about the room again, then pulled London away from the door over toward the cash register. "I really didn't want to tell you this in front of everybody here, but I did want you to hear it from me. I know there's a lot of history between us and that you think I was just using you to get your grandmother's money. That isn't true, London. I loved you. I really honestly loved you."

"Give me a break!"

"I'm not the bad guy here. I wanted to marry you and for us to have a life together."

London could tell by the reaction of the crowd that she and Brenna were the only two people not buying his story. "These people might believe you, but I know you are a damn liar. You withdrew over $20,000 from my bank account and disappeared for two days."

"That money you think I stole from you was for our future. I was down in Kentucky. I'd lined up a new job there I was going to buy a house and surprise you."

"Whatever."

"I'm sorry if I hurt you. I realize that was really dumb."

Looking up at him reminded her too much of the days when they were together. She remembered him taking her in his arms and twirling her around in circles. Then he'd kiss her with her feet nearly eight inches off the ground. She tried so hard to keep those memories distant, but she failed. Feeling defeated, London plopped down in the wobbly wooden bench next to the front door. She absolutely did not believe his story, but everyone else in the room was reacting as though under some kind of magic spell. She spotted question even in Brenna's eyes. She lowered her head and stared at her shoes. The red Nike logo was faded by repeated laundering, the white rubber soles were scuffed, and the ends of her shoes laces were frayed by Vienna's chewing compulsion. She needed a new pair, but these were still comfortable.

"London, I don't want you to hate me," Brody said.

"Why do you care?" She lifted her head and glared at him. His eyes were sullen and dark gray like the sky before a violent thunderstorm.

He hesitated.

"What is it, Brody? Seriously! If you're with somebody else now, then why are you back here bothering me?"

"The person I'm with now is your sister Evie."

The customers gasped in unison, which was an appropriate sound effect for the sensation London felt in her chest as her heart deflated. Not only had he said her sister's name, he had just dashed her hope for justice. She didn't want him. She just wanted him to feel as bad as she did after they first broke up. Instead, she felt like he'd just rejected her again for a second time.

"Wait a minute," she argued. "Geneva knows you're a con man. There's no way she'd go out with you. Besides, I heard a rumor that she's dating Alma-Rae's lawyer."

"First of all, she hates that you refuse to call her Evie."

London chuckled and rolled her eyes. "Boy, you really did your home work."

"Second of all, I am working for Cross, Crenshaw, and Morrissey. The Wickerford's lawyer hired me to do public relations for the Pine Shadows Resort. That's how I met Evie."

"So you just stopped by to tell me you're screwing my sister? Get in line."

"This craziness has to stop, London." Brody grabbed London's wrist. Anger tensed his face and sharpened his words. "She told me about you showing up at Alma-Rae's house the other day like a lunatic and pushing her down on the steps."

"That was a mistake."

"She also told me about your drunken binge and the party you threw at your grandmother's house," he continued. "And you're spreading lies about her just like you did about me."

People were still staring. The wheels of judgment were churning fast like a locomotive and her lying, scheming ex-boyfriend had just tied her to the railroad tracks. She grabbed his arm and led him out to through the double doors. Out of the corner of her eye, she could see the diner patrons gathering at the windows and doorway. Brenna stood just outside the door to keep others from following the couple into the parking lot

"How dare you come to my work and make me look like the bad guy!"

London kicked the ground and sprayed gravel at his feet and ankles. He didn't reply and he didn't retreat.

"She fucks everybody, ya' know. So don't think you're special."

"We're in love, London. And we're getting married."

"This is sick. How long have you two even known each other?"

"Long enough to know that this is real." Brody leaned back against the side of the building as she paced angrily in front of him. "She knows all about our history and what really happened..."

"What really happened? You mean how you conned me out of half my life savings? Did you tell her that part?" London pointed at his car parked a few yards away. "Does she know I bought you that shiny black camero you always dreamed of?"

"Listen!" he demanded. "I'm just here to tell you that you better stop your bullshit with my fiancé. I'm not arguing with you anymore about what happened between you and I. You and I are over. We're history. I'm ready to start my new life with Evie and our baby."

London almost didn't believe the words she was hearing.

"Geneva is pregnant?" Brenna exclaimed.

"That's right," he said. "It's still very early, but I went with her to the doctor last week."

London chuckled. "I think the conman is getting conned by the slut."

"You may have changed the color of your hair, London, but you are still the same hateful person you were when we ended things. I can't believe I ever had feelings for you." Brody pulled the car keys from his pocket and started toward his car.

"The baby probably isn't even yours," she continued. "You're gonna' be stuck raising Denny Chapman's disgusting, evil spawn."

Brody kept walking, stopping only once he'd reached the car. He glared at her from behind the open car door. "You can say whatever you want to me, London. I don't give a damn. But if you ever touch Evie again I will have you arrested."

London picked up a handful of gravel as he sank down into the driver's seat. Brenna grabbed her arm and stopped her from throwing it.

"Let him go, cookie. You're only going to make things worse."

She relented, heeding her friends advice and dropping the rocks. "You're wrong, Brenna. Things can't get any worse."

Chapter Eight

The mountain-guarded boundaries of Coral Leaf always felt like the perfect place for London to hide with her secrets. She wasn't shy, but she was a private person. The root of her dysfunctional relationship with Geneva was jealousy over having to share Grammy's final days, but there was also resentment for the attention she brought to the family's business. London's public confrontation with Brody was just the latest example. She knew she'd face whispers and judgment when she returned into the diner that morning, but she was shocked by the barrage of questions.

People weren't just talking about her relationship with Geneva or her history with the handsome charmer who looked like a slick Hollywood movie star. They were asking about Grammy's estate and how London planned to respond to the Wickerford's offer to buy the property. A few mentioned how the Pine Shadows Resort could put Coral Leaf on the map and bring big money to their humble community, and as the lunch rush crowd funneled in, people were taking sides between London and Alma-Rae. Before Geneva's arrival, few people knew anything about the long-running feud between the Kellers and the Wickerfords, and those who knew didn't really didn't care. Suddenly, her life was front page news. She didn't like it.

London had hoped for a distraction from her growing attraction to Daxter, but she turned out needing him as a distraction from the other drama unfolding in her life. She longed for his straight-forward commentary and blunt disregard for etiquette and being politically correct. The guy was a bad ass. That's what she wanted. That's what she needed. And she wasn't willing to wait for him to make his next move. Her life was already the subject of scrutiny in that town, so why not have a little fun?

Right on schedule Baxter arrived at eleven-thirty. This time she had his BLT and sweet tea waiting for him. When he finished eating, she asked Brenna to cover for her and invited him to join her outside for a cigarette. He told Hadley to head back to the worksite without him, then followed her out to the parking lot without question.

"I have to bum from Brenna," she said, leading him to the far corner of the parking lot where she and Brenna were parked. He followed willingly. "I quit smoking about three weeks ago, but I really need one of these today."

"You do look stressed."

"I feel like I've been run over by a freight train."

"Does it have something to do with the fight people are talking about in there?"

"Oh yea." London took a drag from her cigarette then hopped onto the hood of her car. She adjusted the skirt of her work uniform to help keep the sun baked metal from burning the back of her legs. "You missed a goody."

"Geneva pulling some shit again?"

"Oh, she's topped herself with this one."

Baxter scratched at his thick, scraggly beard. "Does this have something to do with me finding your dog?"

"Not exactly," she said. "But she sent her fiancé down to the diner to scold me for pushing her that night when I went up the hill and accused her of stealing Vienna."

"Who'd marry that?"

London replied with a sarcastic cheerleader head bob. "Ready for the interesting twist?"

Baxter smiled and took a drag from his cigarette. "I'm on pins and needles here, London. Can't you tell?"

"See! I love that cynical, insensitive sense of humor, with just a twinge of hatefulness. Geez, it's perfect. That's exactly what I needed."

"You dragged me out here to tell me I'm hateful?"

London couldn't tell if he was joking or serious. "No. I don't think you're hateful, Baxter. I'm sorry. What I meant to say is that your take on these situations is refreshing. Everybody else is always trying to protect my feelings and make me look on the bright side," she explained, trying to read his facial expression. "Don't get me wrong. I love Brenna to death, but sometimes I need somebody to just agree with me when I say that Geneva is a selfish cunt who rolled into town six weeks ago to cash in on my Grammy's death and run away with my ex-boyfriend. And now he's giving me shit for pushing her down. He's only marrying her cuz she's knocked up and about to be freakin' rich."

"There's a lot of information in that sentence, but okay. I don't use the C word in front of a lady, but yea she's selfish and probably only came to town for the inheritance." Baxter tossed his cigarette and ground it into the gravel with his heavy work boot. "And I get you being fired up about her marrying your ex when we both know that baby probably ain't his. But I don't get what this has to do with me. Do you need me to spy on her or something?"

"No, Baxter. I don't want you to spy," she replied. She slid off the hood and tossed her cigarette on the ground. "I want you to help me forget about them. I want you to help me move on."

"How do I do that?"

London was leaning against the car next to him. He moved closer to her. His blue denim work shirt clung to his sweaty, sticky skin. A first kiss seemed eminent, but the Roger Street Diner wasn't an ideal setting. She turned slightly, leaned her back against the car, and smiled flirtatiously over her shoulder.

"I want you to take me out that date," she said.

Baxter smiled. "Are you sure about that? What about the Wickerfords?"

"I don't care about that anymore."

He took a few steps forward away from the car, hesitating at first with his response.

"Well are you going to do it or not? Don't tease me now, Baxter."

Baxter reached for her hand and tangled his thick fingers between hers. She tilted her head slightly and smiled again as he gently pulled her toward him. His eyes drew her in like a deep blue ocean of intrigue.

"Please tell me what you're thinking," she said.

"I'm trying to figure out what's changed."

"I guess I'm ready to start making my own decisions without worrying about what everybody else gonna' think."

"Not that," he replied, grasping her other hand. "It's that smile. I haven't seen that in a long time."

She sighed. "Are you trying to be romantic?"

"I don't know. I'm not sure I even know how to do that."

"You know how," she insisted. "And you're good at it."

"So this date? You really want to."

"I really, really want to, Baxter."

"I guess we're finally gonna' go out on that date then."

Baxter smiled and pulled her against him. She wasn't sure the gesture qualified as a true hug and he technically never really asked her out, but she wasn't going to complain. Against all odds, London and Baxter were finally making plans for their first date - dinner and a movie on Tuesday night. He seemed nervous or subconscious somehow. Perhaps those months of rejection hadn't prepared him for the real event. London was nervous too, but hers was more like the giddy teenage crush variety. She was excited to find out if he was "built for love".

For the second time that day, London faced a series of questions when she returned inside the diner, except this time she was only being interrogated by her best friend. Brenna didn't ask immediately. She clearly knew better than to ask any questions in front of customers or the other waitress, but as soon as lunch rush was over she escorted London into the ladies room for a private gab session.

"I want details," Brenna insisted, with a broad, devilish smile.

"You look like the Cheshire Cat." London leaned down and checked for feet in either of the two bathroom stalls.

"What are you doing?"

"Making sure nobody else is in here."

"Who cares? Just tell me what happened." Brenna placed her hand on London's shoulder. "You know how I get when you hold out on me."

"Yes, I know. I'm just not ready for the whole world to know that Baxter and I are finally going out on our first date." London pumped her fists in the air triumphantly.

"I knew it!"

"Tomorrow night."

Brenna hugged her friend tightly and cheered with excitement. "I am so proud of you."

"I did it."

"That's right you did it. This is a real victory for you, London. You didn't let that asshole Brody get you down. You went for it," she said, hugging London a second time. "What did he do when you said yes?"

London grabbed a paper towel to wipe down a puddle of water left behind on the sink counter. "Well..."

"You did say yes. Didn't you?"

"I was kind of the asker." London chuckled.

"You asked him out?"

"I asked him to ask me out. Which he didn't really do. He just kinda' said 'I guess we're going out' Then he hugged me... Kind of."

"You two crack me up. Imagine someday telling that story to your grandkids. They'll wonder how you too ever got together."

"Now let's not get ahead of ourselves, Brenna. We haven't even kissed yet."

"But you've been thinking about it haven't you?"

London felt the feverish pink glow lighting up her face, but she said nothing. Brenna didn't have to be a detective to know how she felt about Baxter. London knew that. She was pretty sure her friend knew how she felt even before she did herself. That's why Brenna's prediction about grandkids almost scared the hell out of her. The idea of becoming a parent always made London cringe, but she felt even more strongly opposed to the notion after losing her own mother and grandmother. What if history repeated itself and her kids were left without a mother or father? Who would take care of them?

Sicily's car accident had given London a keen awareness of death and mortality. She was only five years old when her mother died, but she wise enough beyond her years to know death wasn't something to be feared. Her grandparents taught her that death was an inevitable passage and London spent her whole life preparing for it. She was extremely conscientious about her spending. She rented instead of buying a house and paid cash for everything else to make sure Grammy wasn't burdened with any debt when she died. She also never ventured beyond the mighty mountains and hillsides that bordered her little world.

London's paranoia about death probably also explained why her love life, before she met Brody, was limited to casual dating and short-time flings. Her first serious, committed relationship didn't happen until she was almost 30 years old. The notion that she was starting that type of journey with Baxter was somewhat intimidating. Fortunately by the time she reached this realization, it was too late to back out.

The date was set for Tuesday night to coincide with London's day off at the diner. She spent the day primping and mentally preparing. She shaved her legs and painted her toe nails. She took Vienna for a long walk through the woods to clear her mind, then came home to paint her toe nails again and fix the smudges and chips she got from walking through the woods in flip flops. This time she kept her feet propped on the coffee table until the polish was completely dry. Next on her list was a hair color touch up, to hide the dark roots sprouting on top, a long hot soak in the bathtub, then a quick, early dinner so she could eat light during their date.

London admittedly spent an insane amount of time on her make-up, sampling eye shadow colors that would compliment her blue flowered halter dress and trying to figure out which lipstick wouldn't smear when he kissed her goodnight. At the time, the obsession with her make-up seemed a bit unreasonable for a movie night, but she wanted to make a clear distinction between London the woman and London the waitress.

As she wiped away the third and final shade of lip gloss from her make-up bag, she remembered the new lipstick she'd bought weeks ago at the drug store. Brenna had bragged about that brand; she stopped one day on her way from work. She retrieved her purse from the hook on the back of her bedroom door and reached into the inside zipper compartment. No luck. Maybe she was carrying her black purse that day, the one tucked way in the back on the top shelf of her closet. The purse that contained that pink envelope with the embossed roses on the edge. This was the envelope Nurse Wendy gave her at the memorial service. This was her Grammy's final goodbye.

London wasn't ready for that goodbye. Reading that letter would make Grammy's death too real. There would be nothing left to say. She clinched the envelope with both hands and held it close to her chest. She looked up at the heavens with tears in her eyes and apologized aloud to her grandmother. "Not yet, Grammy. I'm sorry. I'm not ready yet." She returned the letter to her black purse, retrieved the lipstick she'd initially been looking for, returned to the bathroom mirror, and tried to set aside that emotion to finish preparing for her date.

Vienna's barking usually announced visitors, but on this night it was the high-pitch squeal from the water pump on Baxter's truck, then the heavy slam of his driver's side door, and then the incessant barking. London spritzed her hair once more with hairspray. The dog perched on the back chair in the front window, still barking at Baxter as he walked from the driveway toward the house.

"Is that your buddy, Vienna?" London patted the dog on the top of her head as she passed through the front room to the foyer. The cuckoo bird emerged from the wooden clock to announce the time as seven o'clock. She flung open the door snickering. "Did you plan that? You're right on..." The sight of him stunned her at first. "t-t-time."

"I knew you'd be shocked."

London stared at him, completely oblivious to Vienna's overzealous greeting for their visitor. "What did you do?"

"I got a haircut. And a shave," he replied.

London didn't know what to say. His bushy beard was gone. His hair was shorter and pulled back into a pony tail, and he was dressed like a business man. Suddenly, her hours in front of the bathroom mirror seemed less ridiculous.

Baxter smiled at the dog jumping up on his leg, then scooped her up from the floor in one arm.

"Oh, Baxter. I'm sorry. She knows better."

"She's cool," he replied, retrieving a plastic baggie from his front pants pocket. "I think she smells the bacon I brought for her."

London tilted her head and smiled. "Who are you?"

"Hey, don't be so surprised. I can be a nice guy. I figure we give her a little treat so she doesn't run away again," he said. "I know my dog always loved bacon."

"I put her little doggy bed in my room. I've started keeping her in there when I'm not home."

"Good idea."

London took Vienna from his arms. "Well, we should probably go so we have time to eat before the movie. The last show usually starts around nine o'clock."

"Okay."

"How do you feel about Italian food?"

"I'll eat anything." Baxter chuckled.

London blushed and shook her head.

"Pervert. That's not what I meant."

"What? No. Nothin'." London turned quickly and headed down the hall with Vienna. Maybe that really wasn't what he meant. Maybe that's just what she wanted him to mean. Maybe she'd gone too long without sex. Maybe he was going to get lucky later that night. Maybe not.

Kenrickson Cove was a major metropolis compared to Coral Leaf and Conners Bluff. The town boasted two gas stations, three taverns, a movie theater, and six different eateries. Gianelli's Italian restaurant was the most popular, especially on the weekends when people from the dry counties in Kentucky came to drink in some of the night life. The food there was so legendary that patrons willingly waited for hours in line for a table on Friday and Saturday nights. The owners eventually transformed the area behind the restaurant into a garden patio with drink and appetizer service, and lighted pavilion for live music. There was a 20 minute wait even on that Tuesday night, so that's where London and Baxter started their date. The music was just getting started for the evening as they took a seat at one of the patio tables.

"I think you'll enjoy them," Baxter said, pointing to the husband and wife duo on the pavilion stage. "They play some times at El Caminos. Mostly folk and country music, but they're pretty good."

London nodded, but said nothing. She was quickly realizing that she was sitting next to a stranger. This wasn't the tough, insensitive man's man she served at the diner every day. This was a gentleman who opened doors for her and pushed in her chair. This was a charming guy who drank Chianti and asked to hold her hand. This was a fun-loving guy sitting on a crowded patio and belting out the chorus to his favorite folk song. She was shocked and strangely disappointed.

"Come on, you know this one," he said, gesturing for her to join in.

"No, that's okay."

Baxter winked at her and continued singing.

London rose from her chair.

"Hey, where ya' goin'?"

"Ladies room." She didn't have the heart to tell him that he was embarrassing her. She didn't really want to start drinking, but she wasn't sure if she was going to make it through the rest of this date without a few cocktails.

The hostess, Felicia, was ready to seat the couple by the time she returned from the restroom. London couldn't help but notice how Felicia was flirting with her man. He did look good in his dark gray dress pants and his neatly pressed shirt. Baxter always wore a blue shirt, but this was the first time London noticed that was the color of his eyes. So he was charming and good looking. That was a bad combination.

"I'm not sure if you got a chance to look at our menu while you were waiting, but we do have some specials tonight. Our penne san ramo - with chicken breast, artichoke hearts, sun dried tomatoes, and peas in a white wine cream sauce. Or our spicy chicken rigatoni," Felicia said.

"That sounds delicious," Baxter replied. "I think I know what I want. Do you need a few minutes, London?"

"The shrimp fra diavolo with the spicy rosa sauce, but just a half order. I'm not really that hungry." London forced a smile for the cute little bimbo with the sunny disposition.

"That's one of my faves," Felicia replied, scribbling on her hand-held note pad. "And what about you, handsome?"

Did she seriously just call him handsome? London wasn't jealous. At this point she was willing to let the cute little bimbo have him, but she should at least get to finish her free dinner first. Baxter smiled back at the waitress, but seemed unimpressed by her sweet talk.

"I'd like the Penne Arrabbiata with the spicy Italian sausage and marinara."

"Ooh, spicy," Felicia flirted.

"London, do you want to split a bottle of Chianti?"

"No thanks. I'll fall asleep during the movie. I'll just have water." What she really wanted was a margarita. She wished she'd picked the Mexican restaurant down the street.

"Maybe that's what I'll do too then. Unless you have sweet tea."

"No, I'm sorry. We have regular tea. There's sugar and sweetener there on the table. We also have Pepsi products."

"Nah, I don't drink soda. I'll just have a glass of tea." Baxter continued talking as the waitress walked away. "It's not the same as when it's brewed into the tea like you guys do it at the diner, but oh well."

"You could have had wine," London said.

"I know, but I was already on my second glass while we were out there waiting. And you're right about the movie."

"What movie are we going to see anyway?"

"I don't know. We can decide when we get there," Baxter said.

Felicia returned right away with their drink order. She handed the glass of water to London then turned her back to her.

"Can I get anything else for you, handsome?" she asked, placing her hand on his shoulder.

"Look, Felicia, you seem like a really nice girl, but so is she," Baxter said, gesturing toward London. "We're on a date here, so I'd appreciate if you'd stop flirting with me in front of her."

Felicia glanced over her shoulder at London, her eyes were misty and a bit glazed. The girl was clearly embarrassed and probably worried about losing out on a good tip. "I'm sorry, miss. I was just trying to be nice and I..."

"It's okay," London assured her.

"I'm sorry, sir. I'm going to go check on your food now," the girl said, quickly disappearing into the kitchen.

"Do you think she's going to spit in our food?" Baxter asked. "That's what you waitresses do sometimes - right?"

"Not all of us." London chuckled, smoothing out a wrinkle in the green and white checked table cloth. "And I don't think you have to worry about her. I think she was more embarrassed than anything else."

"I had to say something."

London nodded and smiled. She was impressed that he defended her honor.

"To be honest, that has never happened to me before." Baxter laughed. "Most women take one look at me and run the opposite direction. Of course, I don't usually dress like this."

"You look really nice," she said. "You clean up good."

"I guess I kind of let myself go after I divorced Brittany," he said. "I was working a construction job down in Kentucky when I met her. We fell in love and got married within a year. Then I found out she cheated on me with half the guys on my crew. This is the first date I've had in three years."

"Wow! She must have really hurt you. I'm sorry, Baxter. I didn't even know you'd been married."

"It was the first one that really hurt," he replied.

Curiosity crinkled the inner corners of her brow. "You've been married twice?"

"I know. Not exactly the kind of thing you're supposed to talk about on a first date."

"I'm sorry. I wasn't judging you," London said. "I'm just really surprised about all the stuff I didn't know about you. I see you at the diner all the time and..."

Baxter interrupted her sentence. "That's when I'm with the other guys from the work site though."

"I know, but still."

"I guess I come across as a real jerk. A real badass?" Baxter shifted uncomfortably in his chair. He pushed his dinner plate forward and folded his arms in front of him on the table.

London didn't have the heart to say yes. She also didn't have the heart to tell him that's why she was attracted to him in the first place and why his kinder, gentler demeanor had her ready to go home. "I'm just surprised to be sitting here talking about relationships. That's all."

"We all have our pasts, London."

"Yes. We. Do." London shifted her eyes away from him and glanced around the busy restaurant dining room. "Where is little miss ray of sunshine with our food?"

Baxter took a swig of iced tea into his mouth then set the glass back down heavy onto the wooden table. "Okay, I guess we won't talk about relationships."

London responded to that comment by changing the subject. "So, where exactly do you live? What part of town?"

"I'm fixing up an old farm house out near Willow River Falls," he replied.

"Really? I didn't think anybody lived out there anymore." All of Coral Leaf was remote, but Willow River Falls was practically deserted 11 years earlier when the dam broke. The river flooded its banks and wiped out the landscape and most of the houses.

"I'm pretty much all by myself out there," he said. "There are a few other houses still left out there, the ones that were on slightly higher ground away from the river, but I don't think anybody lives in them."

"I think people got scared after that. So many people lost everything."

"I wasn't living here at the time, but I've heard about it. I even heard old man Wick had originally picked that place for Pine Shadows."

"Yea, because Grammy refused to sell. They've been trying to get access to the lake since even before Grampy died."

The conversation paused briefly as a different waitress named Veronica arrived finally with their entrees. London unfolded her napkin and placed it across her lap, then gestured for Veronica to refill her water glass. Baxter was eyeing her plate.

"That looks awesome. Is that shrimp still sizzling?"

"I think so," she replied, hoping he wasn't hinting for her to share. She hated that. "Grammy would be proud of me for trying something new tonight. I always order the lasagna when I come here."

Baxter raised his glass and chuckled. "A toast to trying something new."

The waitress chuckled.

London sighed heavily. "You can't toast with iced tea."

"Well, Veronica thought it was funny."

Veronica smiled then tucked the empty serving tray under her arm and walked away.

"Of course she laughed, Baxter. All us waitresses laugh at the smart ass. If we pretend like you're funny we get a bigger tip."

"Whoa! Did I piss you off or something?"

"No. I'm sorry," she replied. She realized that he was probably joking around about how he always ate the same thing for lunch at the diner every day. Spicy sausage penne was quite a departure from his usual BLT. Nevertheless, his lighthearted joke was too much of a departure from the seriousness of her comment about Grammy. "I'm still just a little sensitive about my grandmother. And all this talk about the Wickerfords and ... Well, anyway I'm sorry, Baxter. I didn't mean to snap at you."

"This question probably isn't allowed, but have you even considered selling? Even just part of the land. I don't think Alma-Rae is trying to get rid of you. They just want access to the lake."

"Grammy and Wick despised each other. I couldn't do that."

"So you've thought about it?"

"What is this?"

"What do you mean?" Baxter searched the table top between them. "What is what?"

"I mean what is with the questions, Baxter. Are you still on the clock or something? Trying to get information for Alma-Rae and her greedy posse of lawyers." She jerked the napkin from her lap and dropped it on the table next to her full dinner plate.

Baxter reached across the table and grabbed her hand as she started to stand. "Please don't leave. Come on, London. At least give me a chance to explain."

London pulled her hand away from him and stood up. She started to walk away as planned, but the look in his eyes stopped her. He seemed hurt.

"Please just let me explain," he repeated. He got up and slid his chair around to the side of the table on her right. He placed his hand gently on her shoulder and encouraged her to sit back down. "Just let me say one thing."

"Fine," she grunted, reluctantly taking her seat again.

"Okay. Thank you."

Baxter relaxed back in his chair, still turned slightly toward her. She purposely avoided eye contact.

"Now, don't you think if I was really taking information back to the enemy I would be more sneaky about it?"

"I guess so," London replied quietly, still refusing to look at him.

"I have never once asked you about your grandma's house or any of this real estate business. Not in all the months I've been trying to get you to go out with me on a date. And the only reason I asked about it now is because you seem to be so stressed out about it. I was trying to be helpful. To you. That's all."

London shook her head. She didn't believe him.

"Hey, wasn't I the one who told you Geneva was up to no good?"

She looked up at him, making eye contact again, but still saying nothing. She remembered how she felt about him that day and how impressed she was with his willingness to stand up for her. Even if that meant possibly losing his job.

"I know you don't trust anybody, London. And I don't blame you. Money changes people. But you don't ever have to worry about that with me." Baxter stood up again and moved his chair back to its original spot at the opposite end of the table. "Now, can we please finish our date? My food is getting cold."

Baxter's eyes shifted focus away from London and back to his plate. She watched as he took a bite of his food. And then again as he took a second bite and a third. He said nothing. She said nothing. London felt the urge a few times to apologize, but her pride kept her quiet. They sat like strangers through the rest of their dinner, then Baxter paid the bill and drove her home. They skipped the movie. He didn't walk her to the door. He didn't even shut off the engine as he pulled up to her house. They said goodnight and quickly parted ways. London knew he would never ask her out again. His cold demeanor was definitely warranted. So was her guilt. She just didn't understand the sadness she felt. How could she feel like she lost a friend when he was barely more than just a regular customer at the diner where she worked?

Chapter Nine

Vienna barked happily at London's early arrival home from her date. The dog scratched incessantly against the bottom of the bedroom door until she was released from confinement to greet her long-lost friend. London lifted the cheerful little pooch from the floor, kissed the top of her forehead, and counted her blessings for her joyful reunion with Vienna – the reunion made possible by the man she just rejected. Her rejection was justified; he was being insensitive about Grammy's death and the property dispute. She had every right to fight to keep that land in the family, no matter how much the Wickerfords wanted access to Lake Amethyst. At least that's what she told herself as she recounted the night's events. Had she been unfair to criticize him for not knowing about the back story between old man Wick and her family? She didn't really want to answer that question.

London refilled the dog's water bowl then slipped out of her dress and into a tank top and her favorite pair of lime green shorts. Vienna had quenched her thirst and was pacing by the back door when London returned that short time later. "Come on, baby. Let's go for a little walk now and maybe a ride in Grampy's boat." She grabbed her leash from the hook by the back door, retrieved her flashlight and the keys to her grandfather's boat, and led the dog outside through the screen door.

Confused and guilt-ridden, London stumbled into the night time darkness with her faithful sidekick. The dog focused on the ground beneath their feet, sniffing every blade of grass in search of the perfect spot to relieve herself. London, on the other hand, focused up at the stars. Her grandmother had told her a story once about how the twinkling lights off in the distance weren't actually stars at all. The glow was from millions of tiny televisions for people who had died and gone to heaven; instead of watching news or sitcoms, loved ones could watch their family members still enjoying life. Grammy swore that Sicily was watching when London had her fifth-grade piano recital and when she graduated from high school. Grampy was supposedly up there watching too when London earned her business degree. The notion was crazy to London, even when she was 11 years old, but she suddenly found herself wishing desperately that the story was true. Maybe if Grammy was watching she would have some advice about Geneva, the Wickerfords, and especially about Baxter. The strong, confident facade she'd built to protect herself from creeps like Brody Danbrook was starting to crumble and she needed some help.

As she strolled along her usual path toward the boat house, London heard something rustling behind her. Those woods were always full of critters that roamed at night, but for some reason London was spooked. She sensed danger. Vienna was focused on her business and didn't seem alarmed by the noises. London tried to ignore the sound too, but the rustling got louder and louder. Closer and closer. She could no longer tell whether the noise was ahead or behind her. The light from her flashlight had grown dim. Unsure whether to keep moving forward or run back toward the house, she just told herself to walk faster. Something was in the woods with her. Something big. London pinched the keys between her fingers with the ends pointing out for use as a weapon if needed.

A bright light flashed in her eyes. A man's voice called out to her. She scooped up Vienna from the ground then turned to face the inevitable danger. Her racing pulse pounded in her ears, stifling the sound of his words and disguising his voice momentarily.

"London, it's just me."

"Baxter?"

The light blinded her again as Baxter's flashlight reached out to her in the darkness.

"You scared me to death."

"Sorry, I..."

London interrupted his sentence. "What the hell are you doing here, Baxter?"

"You left this in my truck." Baxter smiled and shone the flashlight on her purse dangling by the shoulder short strap from his thumb.

"Oh," she said. She hadn't noticed before that he was missing the fingernail on that thumb.

There was a brief pause in the conversation as Baxter handed London her purse and seemingly waited for an apology or a thank you. He spoke again just as she realized his intention.

"You're welcome," he said.

"Thank you. And I'm sorry I snapped at you." London looked down and scuffed the dry dirt beneath her flip flops. She couldn't see it in the dark, but she could feel the heavy dust settle atop her toes.

"I guess you're still mad at me about the Pine Shadows shit."

"No, you just scared me."

"Right," he replied sarcastically.

"Seriously. It's kind of creepy out here after dark. I heard something then all of a sudden you were right there behind me and... Well, you know I thought you were some kind of wild animal."

Baxter chuckled. "Or a ghost?"

"I don't believe in ghosts," London replied coldly. She refrained from telling him about her creepy feeling that someone was always watching her and about the series of mysterious dreams and nightmares she'd had since Grammy's death. Some of the most terrifying nightmares took place in those woods between Grammy's house and the lake; those were also some of the strangest. There were several with dark and murderous shape-shifting shadows that hid between the trees and brush. There was also the one with a man-eating shark that jumped out of the creek to grab her as she crossed her Grampy's hand-made wooden bridge. She still wasn't quite ready to believe in ghosts, but something was definitely haunting her.

"Maybe I should walk you home," Baxter said, gently squeezing London's elbow and lighting the pathway behind him with his flashlight.

"Huh?" London pulled her elbow away. "No. I'm not going home. Vienna and I are going for boat ride."

"It's a perfect night for a boat ride," he commented, glancing up at the cloudless sky. "I'll go with you so we can talk."

"That wasn't an invitation, Baxter."

"You didn't let me take you to the movie, so I say we still have a couple hours left on our date."

"The date is over. I apologized. Now please just leave me alone." London let Vienna back down onto the ground and started walking away. She pounded her fist against the bottom of her flashlight hoping to jolt the batteries back to life just long enough to get her to the boat house.

"Don't be that way, London."

She kept walking. No response. She could tell he was following her.

"At least let me walk you down there. You don't even have a working flashlight."

"I have an extra flashlight on the boat." London continued pushing forward without looking back. Baxter's flashlight was lighting her way.

"I can't let you walk out here all by yourself in the dark. It's not safe."

"I've walked this trail a million times, Baxter. I don't need your damn light."

"Trust me, London. I'm trying to help you learn from my mistake about wondering around in the dark," Baxter insisted. "I tripped over an uprooted tree trunk one time on a hiking trip down in Kentucky and broke my leg in three places. I was stranded out there until my buddy came looking for me next morning."

London stopped in her tracks, halting so quickly that Baxter almost ran into her from behind. She wasn't afraid of the dark or the dangers Baxter warned about, but Grammy's favorite saying was echoing in her mind as she stared at their shadow stretched out ahead of them in the band of light. When mistakes of your past cast no shadow on your future decisions, you've been left in the dark. When mistakes of your past cast no shadow on your future decisions, you've been left in the dark . If London rejected Baxter again for the second time that night, she would have been left in the dark. She glanced up at the stars in wonder. Had Grammy just sent her a message? She'd just put new batteries in that flashlight after the night Vienna ran away. How could they go bad so fast? London didn't believe in ghosts or spirits or telepathy or any kind of shit like that. What was happening?

'"Are you okay?" Baxter asked.

She couldn't tell him the truth. "All this stuff with Geneva and the Wickerfords is making me crazy. I don't know how to protect my Grammy's land or her home. But I didn't mean to take it out on you. And I am sorry."

Baxter sighed and raised the flashlight to illuminate his face. "Okay. You're sorry. Now look at my face, London."

London turned her head and glanced at him over her right shoulder.

"You have a right to be pissed off and a little crazy right now with everything that's going on. I don't care if you take it out on me. You can punch, scream, kick, whatever. Just as long as everything you do to me I get to do to that asshole Brody."

London laughed. This was the Baxter she knew from the diner. She'd been waiting for him to show up all night long. "I think you just earned yourself an invitation for a boat ride."

"Alright then," he said, taking Vienna's leash from London's hand. "You lead the way."

Baxter reached his other hand out to London, but she pretended not to notice. Grammy's supposed message said nothing about holding hands. That message also said nothing about letting him drive the boat or dancing with him in the moonlight, but that's what Baxter had in mind when he invited himself on her lake excursion. He insisted, in fact, that he was the captain. London didn't fight him on that point. She preferred to lounge in the back of the boat and enjoy the misty breeze. She had no plans to dance with him though. No way.

Grampy's boat was nothing like the fancy yachts docked at the Kenrickson Cove marina, but the Kellers never lived an extravagant lifestyle. The boat was long enough. The motor was fast enough. The seat cushions were fluffy enough. And the small sleeping cabin below deck was just right. Grampy said he slept there sometimes so he could get up early to go fishing, but London knew the real reason had more to do with Grammy's intolerance for his snoring.

Lake Amethyst stretched across nearly 800 acres, bent between mountains, man-made beaches, and miles of wooded shoreline. London usually stayed near home, but she let the "captain" chart the course that night. There wasn't much traffic on the lake at that hour, so Baxter could explore freely. He sat proudly in the appropriately-named captain's chair, waving happily at the houses and other boats they passed. He looked like a smiley, happy boy leading his own parade. London wanted to find that endearing, but she was annoyed.

Baxter completed a half circle around the lake then stopped in a small fishing cove to join London for some star gazing. He turned on some music, slipped off his shoes, and shuffled toward where she was sitting. She could read his mind. The romantic setting. The music. The sparkle in his eye. The charming grin on his face.

"I'm not sleeping with you," she said.

"Excuse me." He seemed stunned by the accusation.

"You thought you could get me out here all alone under the stars and turn on the charm and I'd sleep with you. It's not going to work, Baxter. I'm not having sex with you."

"I was going to ask you to dance."

London sighed and shrugged her shoulders. "Oh. Well, I'm not doing that either."

"I'm an excellent dancer," he bragged, showing off with a spin on the ball of his foot.

"I don't care. I don't dance."

"Okay. So what do you do for fun?" he asked. "Knock off liquor stores? Terrorize small children?"

"Shut up."

"Hey, I'm just kidding."

"If I'm such a terrible person than why are you even here?"

Baxter sat down on the bench across from her. He leaned forward and flicked the sole of her rubber flip-flop. "Look, we're just talking here. I thought the I hate Baxter part of the date was over already."

London rolled her eyes and grunted in response.

"I like you, London. I'm trying to get to know you better."

"What's the point?" London got up and headed for the captain's chair. "I'm just going to take us back. This isn't going to work out."

"That's it? One lousy date and you're shutting me out again. You are being so childish."

London turned and shouted at him angrily. "I'm childish? You're the..."

Baxter sprang to his feet, met her face to face, and interrupted as she started her tirade. "One minute you can't go out with me because of who I work for. Then you hate all over me because I asked an innocent question about your grandmother's property.   And now you're through with me because I'm too fucking charming."

"Get out of my way! I want to go home."

"I don't think you know what you want."

Baxter grabbed her arms forcefully, pulled her against him, and surprised her with a wet, passionate kiss. His strength and command overwhelmed her and lifted her feet from the floor. London felt fragile somehow squeezed tight against his sturdy frame, disarmed of every defense and every inhibition. She hated him, but that anger only fueled desire for more of his powerful kiss. Her heart raced, her muscles tensed, and the wheels in her mind churned at record speed. She couldn't think clearly. She didn't know what to do. Baxter was right; she had no idea what she wanted.

London had no idea how long she'd lingered there in Baxter's embrace, but she could feel his hands sliding up the back of her tank top. She resisted the urge to let him continue charting his course and finally pulled away. He loosened his embrace. Her feet landed softly back down onto the wooden boat deck. She didn't scold him or ask questions; she assumed he knew he'd crossed the line. London simply broke away from his gaze and started again toward the captain's chair.

"We need to head back now," she said. Her voice was shaky and frail. The taste of his kiss still tingled on her tongue.

Baxter said nothing at first. He sat back down on the cushioned bench and looked up at the sky while London tried to get the boat running. The motor wouldn't start. She tried three times but nothing happened. The lights were still on and the music still played from the onboard CD player, but the motor didn't make a sound when she turned the key.

"What the hell?"

"What's wrong?" Baxter asked.

"I don't know." She tried again, somewhat panicked by the possibility she was stranded on open water with Baxter. Things were too awkward between them after that kiss.

Baxter stood up and crossed the deck toward her. "Can't you get it started?"

"Shit. Shit!"

"It's okay London. Here, let me try."

Baxter grabbed at the steering wheel and nudged her to move out of the way. London shrugged his hand away from her shoulder and squeezed past him. She glanced across the water as Baxter jiggled the keys and tried again to start the lazy motor. She was a strong swimmer. The nearest land was only about 200 yards away, but she had no idea what lurked in those woods.

"I don't seem to be having any luck here either," he said.

"Try again," she insisted.

"No. I think we're stuck."

London cringed. She was convinced this was a set-up, another attempt to get her to sleep with him. "We can't be stuck. Try again."

"I can try all night, London, but it ain't gonna' change nothing. The motor isn't even trying to turn over." Baxter retrieved his cell phone from his pocket and started dialing. "I'll call Hadley or Ralph or one of the guys and see if they know anyone with a boat to pick us up."

"Good thinkin'. Call Harrison at the police station. He has a boat." London read the disappointment on his face as she finished her sentence. "Let me guess. No signal."

"Nada. What about yours?"

"I don't even carry mine except to work. Cell service is really shitty down here." London flung her head backward and sighed. "Dammit!"

"Don't panic. Maybe somebody will come by."

"At ten o'clock on Tuesday night?" London grunted her response. She didn't call him stupid, but her tone certainly suggested the notion.

"It could be worse," he said. "You could be out here all by yourself with a broken down boat."

"Don't get any ideas."

Baxter spun around in the captain's chair and reached for her hand. "That kiss was quite somethin'. Like the fourth of July all over again."

London rolled her eyes and pulled her hand away. "Maybe for you."

"You kissed me back."

"So what?" She tossed her hands up in the air dramatically.

"You liked it."

"So what?" She couldn't think of a better response and she knew a lie wouldn't be convincing at this point.

Baxter leaned forward, smiling at her. "You already said that."

London spun around and stepped away; she couldn't look at him.

"What? Are you ashamed that you liked it?"

"No." That was the truth.

London took a seat on the long cushioned bench that ran the length of the stern. Baxter moved from the captain's chair and stood before her. He smiled down at her with a victorious glimmer in his eyes.

"So you did like it," he declared. He sat down next to her and rested his head on the upper cushion. "I knew you liked it. You can't kiss like that unless you mean it."

"Big deal. So I liked it. So you're a good kisser."

Baxter corrected her. "I'm a great kisser."

"Whatever," she grumbled, bobbing her head from side to side trying to convey a nonchalant attitude.

Baxter wasn't even looking at her and he didn't respond further to her comment. He kept his head tilted back and his eyes closed. She stared at him, then up at the stars, and then stared back at him one more time. Just like his usual comments at the diner, Baxter's statement was presumptuous and borderline ridiculous, but the conviction in his voice made her stop and think. She and Brenna called that quality "silly arrogance." Brenna meant it as an insult, but for London that was an attractive quality. She admired his confidence, even though at the moment he was making her crazy.

Chapter Ten

The moonlit water splished and splashed softly against the sides of the boat. A gentle breeze rustled the tree branches. Owls hooted. Crickets chirped. The last song had finished playing on the CD player and Baxter was taunting London with the silent treatment. Perhaps he had learned through observation that arguing only hardened her stubborn defenses. Crying didn't work either, except for with Grammy or Vienna. The silent treatment almost always compelled an apology, even when she wasn't truly sorry. That was the case on this night; she was too intrigued by his behavior and too confused by her own emotions.

London couldn't remember the first time they met. His neanderthal, sexist attitudes and un-kept appearance helped him blend in with most of the other regulars at the diner. She did remember though the first time he asked her out on a date that previous November. Much to Calvin's chagrin, she and Brenna had decided for Halloween to dress up as roller derby chicks - complete with hot pants, roller skates, broken teeth, and black eyes. The costume was Brenna's idea, but London was easily convinced. At that time she was trying to catch the attention of a gorgeous FedEx delivery driver named Pete. As it turned out, Pete was more into Claudia's Marilyn Monroe costume. That night after work, London made a stop at the drug store then went straight home and dyed her hair blonde. Baxter commented the next day that Pete was a fool and that he thought she was beautiful no matter how she wore her hair. Then he asked her for her phone number. She had no idea she'd end up in this position eight months later, stranded alone with him on the lake in the middle of the night. She wondered how she'd kept his interest for so long.

"I guess I've been kind of hateful tonight. Huh?" she asked.

Baxter opened his eyes, but didn't look directly at her. "No more than usual really."

"Wait a minute," she stuttered.

"I'm joking." He chuckled, interrupting her thought process as she revved up the resentment engine. "You aren't hateful."

"That isn't funny. I was trying to apologize."

Baxter turned sideways, resting his left knee on the bench in front of him. "I was just trying to break the tension." He touched London's right shoulder as he continued his response. "You don't have to apologize, London. I know you better than you think I do. And I get it."

"I swear sometimes you sound like a stalker."

"See, I understand comments like that too." He scooted closer. "I know that you don't trust me and I don't blame you. That asshole ex-boyfriend of yours ruined that for you. And all this shit with your grandma's land and Geneva is enough to make anybody crazy."

London sighed. "That's the truth."

"I know how money changes people, London. I've seen it. I've lived it."

London glanced at him curiously over her shoulder.

"That's what I was trying to tell you earlier when I was talking about my first wife. I bet you won't believe this, but I actually come from money. My daddy was a very rich man."

"I didn't know that."

"Oil wells down there in Texas."

London turned slightly. She inadvertently put her hand on his knee. "If you're rich then what are you doing working for the evil Wickerford family? You should be building your own summer resort."

"I'm not rich," he said.

"But you..."

"I said my daddy is rich. I haven't seen my parents since I was 19 years old."

London folded her legs beneath her and listened intently as Baxter described his first wife Hillary, and the single decision that ended their marriage and estranged him from his family. Hillary Rhoetinger was Baxter's girlfriend during all four years of high school. They graduated together in the summer 1995 and got married when Baxter got ready to leave for college in Austin, six hours away. His father had big plans for Baxter in his thriving oil company, but first a degree in finance and an MBA. He loved his bride, but he hated school. He barely survived the first semester and had to break the news to his dad that he wouldn't be enrolling for a second term.

"My father looked me square in the eye and said that no son of his was going to be a college drop-out. When I reminded him that he never went to college either, he smacked me with the back of his hand and told me to go back to Austin and my white trash whore of a wife or he'd disown me."

London gasped. "He called her a white trash whore?"

"I told him to go to hell." Baxter got up from his spot on the bench and paced uncomfortably in front of her. The story had obviously evoked some bitter emotions. "Then I went to the only bar in town that would serve an underage kid and I got drunk. By the time I made it back to Austin the next day, Hillary was gone. I guess all she cared about was the money."

"Oh, Baxter. I am so sorry."

"I got the annulment papers the same day I got the eviction notice from the apartment landlord. My father had the lease cancelled."

"They threw you out on the street? Where did you go?"

"I stayed with friends for a while. Moved around a lot, working odd jobs until I finally found my first construction gig." Baxter sat back down in the captain's chair and started laughing. "I can't believe I'm telling you this, but I was actually a singing telegram clown for a while."

London laughed, pulling her hands up to cover her mouth as she pictured the scene.

"I had the squeaky red nose and everything," he added.

"You probably should have kept that to yourself," London said, laughing with Baxter as he buried his face in his hands. As the laughter subsided though, she recognized why he shared such an intimate detail of his life. He did understand what she was going through and he'd let himself be vulnerable to prove that to her.

Baxter looked up at her as she approached him from the other side of the boat, but he said nothing more. His eyes were dry, but she could sense his strong urge to cry. He was probably too proud to shed tears in front of a woman.

"I'm sorry that happened to you, Baxter," she said. She crouched down in front of him, wrapped her arms around his torso, and rested her head on his chest.

"I'm sorry that happened to you too, London." He squeezed her tightly and gently kissed the top of her head, but only let her linger in his embrace for a few seconds before nudging her away. "Now let's see if I can get this boat motor going again."

"Okay. I'm going to go check on Vienna."

London wasn't concerned at all about the dog sleeping comfortably below deck, but she thought Baxter needed some privacy. He reminded her of her Grampy at that moment. He used to work on the boat when overwhelmed with emotions too because he was too proud to let anyone see him cry.

When London returned above deck a few minutes later, Baxter had given up trying to get the motor running and had opened a couple beers. By this time, the moon was no longer visible from where the boat had drifted. He couldn't see well enough in the dark to try anything more than what he'd done already.

"I hope you don't mind. I figured since we're not going anywhere I'd grab a couple of brews from the little mini fridge."

"Oh, you found the fridge?"

"I was looking for a life boat, lifted up the seat cushion and there it was," he replied. "Pretty clever hiding it in the bench there. Huh?"

"Grampy loved that hidden cooler. Grammy always got mad at him if he drank beer on Sundays, so he used to sneak out here on the boat for a cold one. Grammy knew though. It was hard to get anything past her." London laughed as she remembered the silly arguments between her grandparents. "If I ever get married I want to have a relationship just like theirs."

London froze. Where did that comment come from? Twenty minutes ago she wanted to throw this guy overboard and suddenly she was talking to him about marriage. She was so confused. She chugged her beer, trying to think of something else to say - anything else that would change the subject. Too late. She didn't think fast enough.

"I'd like to get married again," Baxter said.

"I guess it would be nice to have somebody cook, clean, and do laundry for you."

Baxter grabbed her foot and tugged playfully as though he was going to pull her off her bench. "That isn't the reason, smart ass."

They laughed.

"Seriously, I'd like to have somebody to travel with and somebody soft and sweet smelling to snuggle up with every night when I go to bed."

London blushed. "And what exactly do you mean when you say snuggle?"

Baxter moved closer. "I mean snuggle, but if you want to talk about that other thing..."

"No. That's okay," she interrupted. She held out her arm to block him as he moved in still closer. "I wouldn't want to lead you on."

"We have plenty of time for that later I guess," he said. "But what about traveling? Do you like to travel?"

"No. I've never been anywhere other than West Virginia."

"Oh, I'll have to take you on a trip some time," he insisted.

Baxter kicked up his feet and started listing all the places he'd lived around the country. He was born in Arizona, but moved to Texas when he was seven. Then he lived in Oklahoma, Arkansas, Kentucky, and eventually West Virginia. He and his dad went to Canada every year on fishing expeditions. He took Hillary to Hawaii for their honeymoon and to Florida with Brittany. His list seemed endless. London eventually lost track and lost interest. Baxter noticed apparently.

"Am I boring you?"

"No. Sorry. It's just hard for me to imagine all these places exist beyond these hills." London yawned. "What time is it anyway? I'm really getting tired."

"One-thirty. Still four more hours until sunrise. I think once I've got some good daylight I'll be able to fix the motor and get you home."

"I don't think I'm gonna' make it another four hours," she said, yawning again. "Damn, I am so sleepy. Maybe I shouldn't have drank this beer so fast."

"I'll be okay up here if you want to catch a few winks." Baxter patted the cushioned seat next to him. "These benches seem comfy enough. I'll probably try to get some sleep too."

"Maybe I should get some sleep. I might have to swim for it in the morning if I'm going to make it back to work on Thursday."

"I'll get the boat fixed. I promise," he said.

London thanked him and said goodnight, then made him promise not to try sneaking into bed with her in the middle of the night. She felt guilty for making Baxter sleep above deck, but neither one could be trusted to share that tiny bed in the sleeping quarters below.

Despite their unusual circumstances and the awkward tension between her and Baxter, London fell asleep fast and slept soundly through the night. She awoke the next morning with only little Vienna curled up tightly in the small of her back. She could tell it was morning by the daylight visible around the edges of the sleeping cabin door. She didn't remember closing that door; she'd gone to bed that night secretly hoping Baxter would break his promise. Perhaps he closed the door.

Baxter was still stretched out on his back, sleeping shirtless on the bench at the back of the boat. London stood for a moment and stared. He looked just as delicious as he had in her fantasy, minus the wicked dragon tattoo. She admired the strong muscle tone in his arms and upper body, and the glistening beads of sweat in the thin patch of hair on his chest. She tried not to notice how snugly his pants fit in the front, but the sun shone down like a spotlight on her secret desire. The sight of him excited her and inspired her imagination. She had to look away. She needed to focus instead on the beautiful nature that surrounded them.

The boat had drifted overnight, so London was confused and disoriented at first by what she saw. The clubhouse. The Wickerford mansion on the hill. Familiar sites of home from every angle. They were adrift in the reflection of Mount Karma, but how could that be? How could that boat drift more than three miles in just a few hours and end up there in Grammy's final resting place?

London gasped aloud. "This is impossible. This is impossible," she murmured. The shock spun her into circles on the boat deck. She pinched herself repeatedly. This had to be another dream. Vienna peeked up at her from the sleeping cabin entryway, but quickly disappeared back down the steep, narrow staircase.

Baxter awoke, stirred by the commotion and panic in London's voice. He called out to her, but she was too upset to answer at first. He got up from his resting spot and tried to physically console her. "London, what's wrong? Are you okay, London? London?"

"What did you do?" she squeaked, bracing the sides of his face with her hands. "Did you move us? Did you move the boat?" Her eyes pleaded. Her heart raced. This was impossible. She mumbled repeatedly. "Le Coeur du Lac. Le Coeur du Lac."

"What are you talking about, honey?" Baxter stroked her hair. "You're scaring me, London. What's going on sweetie?"

"Did you move the boat, Baxter? Last night while I was sleeping?"

"No. How could I move the..." Baxter paused for a moment as London continued rambling. "What is Le Coeur du Lac?"

London froze, lost in his eyes. Part of her panic was the fear that he was tricking her or trying to manipulate her somehow, but she could see the truth in his expression. He had no idea what she was talking about. She'd never mentioned Le Coeur du Lac or told him anything about her mother's painting. When she finally explained that the heart of the lake was the final resting place for her grandmother, grandfather, and mother, Baxter seemed equally shocked by the coincidence.

Baxter sat back down on the bench and stared blankly at London. "Is somebody trying to tell us something?"

"I don't believe in this kind of stuff, Baxter. I just don't." London pinched herself again, harder this time. This wasn't a dream.

"How do you explain us drifting all the way..."

"I can't explain it," she replied, interrupting his question. "It's impossible."

London crumbled to the floor with her legs folded neatly beneath her. Tears streamed down her face and she sobbed. She was sad, frightened, and confused. She'd asked her grandmother for a sign, but never expected any response. Like she told Baxter, she didn't believe in that kind of stuff.

Baxter moved onto the floor of the boat and scooted close to London with his legs folded in front of her. He wrapped his arms around her sympathetically and softly kissed her forehead. She clung to him, guided by urges that were not her own. They were in the midst of something powerful. She couldn't see it, but she sensed it. She couldn't hear it, but she understood the message. London could no longer ignore that her Grammy was communicating to her. Her concern for her granddaughter had transcended the boundary between life and death to ensure London didn't miss this opportunity. Her grandmother's advice echoed in the quiet awkwardness of Baxter's embrace. Open your heart. Let people in.

London surprised Baxter with a sultry kiss on his neck. She dug her fingers deep into the flesh on his back and kissed his neck again. He pulled back and gazed at her hungrily as she unfolded her legs and moved to straddle herself across his lap. He guided her gently forward with his hands on her hips, then helped her slip her tank top over her head. She said nothing. He said nothing. They kissed wildly and passionately, grinding against each other in a feverish rhythm. London could feel his excitement pressed against her, straining against every thread of clothing that kept his wand from the magical kingdom.

Tiny beads of sweat formed on her tingling flesh. She tilted her head back, savoring the sensation of his hot kisses trailing down her neck. He lifted her effortlessly and in one fast, fluid motion repositioned her on her back. He continued his kisses toward her navel and to points further south as he removed her favorite lime green shorts. The rough texture of his unshaven face tickled the inside of her thighs as he explored territory other men had searched for but never discovered. This was no fantasy. Those shockwaves she felt were very real. London was in love. Baxter was just getting started.

The heat of the mid-summer sun cooked the hard wooden floor beneath them and soon urged the lustful lovers into the comfortable bed below deck. They made love for hours, uninhibited by hunger, thirst, or fatigue. Baxter knew how to pleasure a woman and his stamina was quite impressive. The passion and intensity overpowered her defensive instincts and freed her heart from its protective cocoon. Her muscles tensed. Her mind surrendered. Her body succumbed to that glorious, magnificent vibration. And she cried.

Tears of angst, grief, joy, and every other possible emotion were streaming down her face as London flung her head back onto her pillow.

"Are you okay?" Baxter asked. "Why are you crying?"

"Don't worry. I'm just a little overwhelmed," she whimpered. "We should have done that a long time ago. I had no idea."

"Hey, don't blame me. I was trying," he joked.

London responded with a breathless chuckle.

Baxter kissed her forehead and began to rise from the bed. "You rest now. I'm going to try to get us home."

London didn't care whether they ever returned to dry land; the realities of life were far less appealing than the private fantasy land she discovered there between the sheets. Nevertheless, her sense of responsibility ultimately prevailed. More than 10 hours had passed since their departure from the dock and Vienna was clearly ready to go home to her grassy backyard. Fortunately for the desperate little doggy and her small bladder, Baxter identified the source of their problem quickly; it was a loose spark plug he couldn't see in the nighttime darkness. He seemed slightly embarrassed by the ease at which the problem was fixed, but not at all dissatisfied with the events that transpired as a result of his earlier oversight. Within minutes the motor was running again and they were making their short journey back to the clubhouse.

Neither said much as they tracked back through the wooded trail to London's house. She was physically and emotionally exhausted and uncertain about his expectations regarding their relationship. There was obviously mutual attraction and great chemistry, but for the first time in a long time, she wanted something more meaningful than casual sex. She was invested at this point and afraid to ask if he felt the same way. That warm, tender goodbye kiss might be their last. She tried to savor it.

At 32, London felt like she was past the appropriate age for bragging to her girlfriend about her latest sexual encounter, but she knew Brenna wasn't beyond the age for asking questions even at 37. The markings Baxter left on her neck were too obvious. As she soaked in her warm, bubbly bath water and reminisced about the best sex of her life, she contemplated what she was going to tell her best friend. To anyone else, the story about the stranded boat and the mysterious beyond-the-grave message from her grandmother would have seemed crazy, but Brenna knew London's feelings on the subject. She was a diehard skeptic about those kinds of stories and would never make such a claim unless there was no other possible explanation. London still had doubts, but Le Coeur du Lac was Grammy's resting place. That wasn't a coincidence.

London arrived for work on schedule the next morning at five-thirty. She wore a festive Fourth of July bandana around her neck, but that didn't hide the giddy grin that gave away her secret. Brenna seemed to know instantly. The interrogation began as soon as Calvin disappeared into the kitchen.

Brenna leaned against the counter where London was stationed with a stack of menus needing an updated daily specials page. She smiled triumphantly. "I was going to ask how your date went, but you don't have to say a word."

"What are you talking about?" London fidgeted with her scarf.

"Don't play dumb, London. You are in love."

"I'm not in love," she insisted. Those feelings were stirring, but she was trying to stay in denial about that until Baxter revealed his own intentions. She knew the only way to get

Brenna off the subject though was to confess that they'd slept together. "Come on. Time for a cigarette break."

Brenna did not argue. She followed London out to their cars at the edge of the parking lot continuing the discussion as they walked. "You are in love, London. I can see it in your eyes."

"I'm not in love. I'm just satisfied."

"Satisfied?" Brenna tapped her finger against her mouth and repeated the word. She had a confused glaze in her eyes.

"Yes. You know... Satisfied."

"Oh, you mean satisfied." Finally Brenna understood. "You slut."

"Hey!"

"I can't believe you slept with him," Brenna exclaimed.

London hung her head and sighed. "I knew I shouldn't have told you."

"I'm your best friend. You're required by law to tell me. I'm just shocked. How did it happen?"

"Well, the boat motor quit on us and we were stuck out on the lake..."

"So you got bored?" Brenna turned back toward the car and reached for her cigarettes off the front dash.

"No! Will you just stop so I can tell you?"

"Sorry sorry sorry. Tell me."

"The boat broke down in Le Coeur du Lac."

Brenna dropped her lighter and glared at London in disbelief. "Oh my God. That's a sign. You were just driving along and..."

London interrupted to clarify. "Oops. No. The boat actually broke down in a little fishing cove on the other side of Mount Karma. We drifted overnight to Le Coeur du Lac."

"Are you sure about that? Maybe Baxter was just playing a trick on you."

"I thought that at first too," London said, finally lighting the cigarette she'd had dangling from her lips. "but Brenna, he doesn't know anything about Mom's painting or anything. I never told him. You never told him. Right?"

Brenna shrugged.

"Calvin and Geneva are the only two other people who know about that place. Calvin wouldn't tell. And Baxter hates Geneva. Plus I would have heard the motor running. I was sleeping down below deck."

Brenna flicked ashes from her cigarette then hopped onto the hood of her car. "That's just really odd. How could the boat drift that far?"

"That's my point. It's like you said. It was a sign," London insisted. Her eyes bulged with excitement and disbelief as she recounted the whole story. She started her story talking about her initial disappointment at the restaurant, continued through the take-charge kiss before she fell asleep, and ended with the moment she realized where they were. "I really really really think my Grammy was trying to talk to me. She was trying to tell me that he's the one."

"I've been telling you that for a month. You wouldn't listen to me," Brenna joked.

London tossed her spent cigarette and squashed it into the gravel. "Don't tease."

"I'm sorry, London. So tell me. How was it?"

"The best I've ever had," she confessed.

Brenna giggled and kicked her feet out in front of her. London joined in the laughter, moving quickly from in front of the car bumper to avoid getting kicked. This was the exact reaction she expected and hoped for.

"Cookie got herself some good lovin'. Woo hoo!" Brenna cheered. "It was probably so good cuz of all that pent up sexual tension from you playing hard to get for so long."

"It was a lot of things. A lot of things for a very very long long time."

"You are so damn lucky. Seth and I have been married so long that he's finished in like two and a half minutes flat. And that's when the baby isn't screaming and Libby doesn't have two hours worth of homework and the dish washer doesn't need to be unloaded and..."

"I get it," London interrupted. "It also helped that we were stranded in the middle of a lake with nothing better to do."

Brenna hopped down off her hood, took a final drag from her cigarette, and started leading London back into the diner. She was smiling and shaking her head. "This is such an incredible turn of events, Cookie. I'm so happy you have a boyfriend again."

"I don't know yet if he's officially my boyfriend, but I am happy that I decided to go out with him. Grammy would be proud. Well, except for the reckless, impulsive sex thing." London laughed. "Maybe now I can chill out about all this stuff with Geneva and Brody."

"I wasn't going to mention his name," Brenna said. She opened the heavy red metallic door and gestured for London to lead the way back into the diner. "But that is definitely the best part of all this."

Claudia was just inside the door spreading a clean table cloth onto the front booth table. "Best part of all what?" she pried.

"Were you eavesdropping?" Brenna accused.

"I was just asking a question. Gee whiz."

"It's okay, Claudia. We were just talking about my sister."

"Oh, I heard she was pregnant. I bet you are freaked out."

London didn't explain to Claudia that the pregnancy was old news. In fact, she purposely misled her to believe that was exactly what they were talking about. Geneva's baby seemed to be the popular topic of conversation that day anyway, second only to London's bombshell confrontation with Brody there at the diner during her last work shift. Some of the regulars offered sympathy to London, accusing Geneva of stabbing her in the back. Others who saw the argument were more sympathetic to Brody and intent on celebrating the baby's impending arrival. Thanks to London's compulsive need for privacy, she made no attempt to defend herself as they rehashed the couple's bitter history. She was more focused on the future, like Baxter's anticipated arrival at the diner in three hours, 43 minutes, and 12 seconds.

Chapter Eleven

Baxter arrived on schedule at eleven-thirty, but he avoided his usual seat at table 6. Instead, he scooted into the booth at table 11 on the other side of the dining room. London fretted, interpreting this choice as a bad sign for their future together. The worry subsided quickly though as she considered that table 11 was still in her section and that the Roger Street Diner was not the only place for lunch. Nearby in Kenrickson Cove there was Giovanni's, The Brothers Brothers Sandwich shop, Abby's Home-style Buffet, and a few fast food restaurants. He wouldn't be there at all if he wanted to avoid her.

Hadley and Marco showed up as London finished keypunching the order for table 8 into the point of sale register. She poured two glasses of sweet tea for Baxter and Hadley, and crossed the dining room to take their order. Hadley was questioning Baxter about the seating choice as she approached.

"Is there something wrong with our usual spot?"

"You got a problem with a change of scenery?" he replied, jabbing Hadley with his elbow as he tried to scoot in next to him. "Sit on the other side, bro."

As Hadley sat down, Marco draped his left arm around his shoulder and gave him a noogie. "Isn't this romantic?"

"Knock it off," Hadley demanded. He opened his silverware packet and checked his reflection using a butter knife. "Don't screw with my hair, dude. I have a date later."

London handed Hadley his glass of tea, laughing at the boys' juvenile antics. She set the other on the table in front of Baxter, purposely avoiding eye contact. She was thrilled to see him, but still very nervous about the verdict she awaited. She'd forgotten about the emotional rollercoaster ride that went along with the prospect of falling in love.

"Welcome back, Marco. What brings you to town this time?"

"Construction starts on the hotel in two weeks. We have to get the mountain ready."

London wasn't quite sure what that meant, but she decided not to ask. "What can I get you to drink?"

"I'll take sweet tea too," Marco replied.

"Let me go grab that while you figure out what you want. I'll be right back."

Baxter reached out to her and grabbed her arm at the elbow. "Wait. No. Here, let him have this one. I think I'm going to order something different today," he said, sliding the other glass of tea across the table.

She tilted her head and smiled at him. How could a simple squeeze on the elbow excite her so much? And what was he doing changing his drink order?

Baxter smiled back at her and nodded his head. "That's right. I want a Pepsi today instead."

"Really?" Hadley asked.

"First the table and now this? You don't even like soda," London said.

"We haven't even finished giving you shit about the haircut and shave yet," Marco teased.

London bobbed her head and giggled. "Yea. What's next, Baxter? Are you going to tell me you don't want a BLT?"

"I was gonna' wait until you got back with my Pepsi, but okay. Yes. I want the country fried steak sandwich today," he said.

London glanced at Hadley. He looked equally puzzled. "Did he get hit in the head or something today?"

Hadley shrugged.

"My head is just fine," Baxter insisted, sliding his hand down from her elbow to grab her hand. "I'm just trying to prove to my girlfriend that I can change. I can try new things."

Calling her his girlfriend was presumptuous, but that was Baxter's nature, just as it was usually London's nature to challenge such bold declarations. Before she could respond to this statement or the hand-holding, Baxter boosted himself up, kneeling his right leg on the red vinyl booth seat, and kissed her. He didn't let doubt cast shadow on his confidence. Even after months of rejection, he had remained unphased by the obstacles London tried to put between him and what he wanted. That strategy had already gotten her into bed once, even though she would never admit that aloud.

Baxter winked and pinched her bottom as she pulled back slightly. She was sure the gasps and whispers from behind her were related to that kiss. She didn't realize that Geneva and Brody had walked in until she heard Claudia congratulate them.

"Oh shit," Hadley said.

"Do you want me to..."

London interrupted Baxter. She knew what he was preparing to offer. She didn't want his help. "Excuse me. I just need to take care of something real fast." She could hear Hadley explaining to Marco as she walked away that the two sisters hated each other.

Brody and Geneva had taken a seat at the counter where Claudia was working that day. Brody ordered a ginger ale for himself and an orange juice for his pregnant fiancé. "We just stopped by to talk to London for a minute," Brody explained.

"What do you need to talk to me about?"

"I need to get some of my things from the house," Geneva said. "And my key doesn't work."

"Probably because I changed the locks yesterday," London replied coldly.

"You have no right to do that. That house is half hers." Brody completed the full spin on his stool and stood up. He stared down at London as if trying to intimidate her.

"Don't make trouble, honey. I don't want to make a scene. I just need to get my things."

Baxter had crossed the room to help as well by this time. He and Brody both puffed out their chests and stared each other down, but neither seemed intimidated by the other. "Is there a problem here?"

"There's no problem," London insisted. "Geneva and her conman boyfriend can't seem to understand why I would feel the need to change the locks on my grandmother's house."

Geneva rolled her eyes.

"Haven't you taken enough from me, Brody?"

"London, please stop," Geneva insisted. "I just need my things. We're going to California for a couple weeks with Alma-Rae. I need my big suitcase and the rest of my clothes. The guys from Marco's company said we can't stay in the house until they're done with the blasting."

"Blasting?" London asked.

"They finally got all the trees cleared, now they have to level off some of the mountain surfaces to start building the hotel."

London looked at Baxter. "That's what Marco was talking about."

He nodded.

"And they said you have to get out?" she asked.

"You should probably go too, London, just to be safe," Baxter said. "I was getting ready to tell you that."

London looked to her friend, standing nearby eavesdropping and pretending to wipe down a table. "Well, Brenna I guess I'm going to be staying with you for a little while."

"As long you need to, Cookie."

"So how about it, London. Can I get the key?" Geneva asked. "Please?"

"I only have one set," London replied. "But I get off work here at three-thirty. You can come by the house around four o'clock and pick up your stuff then."

"Okay," Geneva agreed.

"Why don't we meet you here at three-thirty then drive over to Dillan's Hardware Store and get copies made? Geneva deserves her own set of keys to her grandmother's house."

London wanted to argue, but she could see Calvin through the kitchen pass-through window and he was nodding his head, urging her to agree. The reverend usually minded his business, so when he expressed an opinion – even a subtle opinion – she listened.

"Fine. Three-thirty," London grunted. "Don't be late."

"Fine," Geneva said.

Brody put his arm around Geneva and helped her off her stool. He placed a five dollar bill on the counter, told Claudia to keep the change, then pushed past Baxter, deliberately running into him.

London sighed heavily as the heavy aluminum door slammed behind them. She bit down hard on the inside of her cheek to keep from screaming at Claudia when she commented that Geneva and Brody made a cute couple. Her brain was over stimulated and already overreacting to her new boyfriend's need to take care of her, her ex-boyfriend's obvious jealousy, and her own concerns about that man having access to her home again. She was ready to volunteer to help Marco blast Mount Karma; her head was about to explode anyway.

Brody Danbrook was gifted in his abilities to win peoples' approval. Aside from his charms and good looks, there was some kind of relatable factor or something that made folks like him; sometimes they didn't even know why. He likely missed his calling as a politician. There were certainly 25 or 30 people in that dining room that day that would have voted for him. The only question at this point was whether Geneva shared that same gift or if she was just the benefactor of Brody's influence. She had certainly gained sympathy with her soft-spoken "we don't want any trouble" pleas about the house keys and their combined efforts had, within 10 minutes, spoiled Baxter's first public kiss and turned some of London's friends against her. The overtly masculine tension between Brody and Baxter only added more flames beneath the giant black witch's pot.

Baxter had a powerful gift too, but unlike Brody his special talent was alienating people. His new clean-shaven appearance had gained him a few popularity votes, but London sensed some unease in peoples' minds about their budding relationship. Some of that had to do with London's own reluctance at the beginning, but their continued disapproval seemed to have more to do with the Baxter-to-Brody comparison. She overheard Kelly Giles whisper that she had traded in a smoking hot Ferrari for a 1977 Ford Pinto. London tried to ignore the hateful commentary. After eight months of indecision, she had no regrets about becoming his girlfriend. Baxter was one of the few people still defending her in the ongoing war and the need for his protection was becoming more dire.

The diner's accountant, Wade Forrester, stopped at the diner every Thursday afternoon for lunch with his elderly mother. The house-key controversy was just subsiding when he and Mrs. Forrester entered the restaurant. Baxter had returned to his table, Claudia had shut up about the cute couple, and London's blood pressure was coming back down.

Brenna escorted Wade and his mom to their table. London was standing a few feet away refilling Hadley's iced tea glass. Wade started asking her about her car.

"London, isn't that your little red Mazda out there in the parking lot?"

"The old Miata convertible? Yea, that's mine. Why?"

"I wouldn't drive that thing," he said.

London chuckled nervously. That seemed like such an odd statement. "Why not?"

Baxter chimed in too. "What are you talking about?"

"I noticed something leaking underneath the front. It looks to me like brake fluid," he replied. "It's all over the gravel under there. You don't have any enemies do you?"

Brenna gasped. "Wade, that isn't funny."

"I wasn't trying to be funny."

Brenna grabbed London's arm as Baxter and Hadley sprung from their seats to go check it out.

"I didn't mean to freak everybody out. I just didn't want you to get hurt," Wade added.

London patted him on the shoulder, but couldn't mutter the words thank you. She was in shock. She thought that kind of thing only happened in movies and cliché crime dramas. Geneva was not above suspicion. Neither was Brody. Brenna asked Claudia to cover while she and London joined the guys out back in the parking lot. Calvin and a few other diner patrons followed too.

Hadley was laying under the car. Baxter was retrieving a flashlight from the big metal utility chest in the bed of his truck.

"Can you see anything?" London asked.

"It's not your brakes. Brake fluid isn't green," Hadley yelled. "It's power steering fluid. I'm just trying to figure out how it's leaking."

Baxter kneeled and handed him the flashlight, then returned his attention to London staring nervously. "It's okay, London. It isn't the brakes, honey. Nobody's trying to kill you."

London couldn't tell if that was sincerity or sarcasm, but she didn't care. She wasn't going to rule out anything until Hadley came back with his verdict. Hadley was a former mechanic. Baxter couldn't even figure out a loose spark plug on the boat.

"Do you want me to call Troy over at the garage?" Calvin asked. "We can get the car towed over there and checked out."

Hadley's head reappeared from beneath the car. "That's probably a good idea, Calvin."

"What is it?" Brenna asked, clinging tightly to London's hand.

"I can't see anything, but it's definitely power steering fluid. I'm sure it's nothing major, but Troy can put it up on the lift and check it out for you."

"He's a good man," Calvin assured her. "I'll go in and call him now."

Calvin walked back toward the diner, followed by a few grumbling onlookers who seemed disappointed that London's brakes hadn't been cut. Surely nobody had turned against her to the point of wishing her that kind of misfortune; there was just a strong appetite for drama. This day had already exceeded the threshold for drama.

"Come on, Cookie. Let's get back in there before Claudia has a meltdown," Brenna suggested.

Baxter wrapped his arms around London and pulled her into an embrace, at the same time tugging her hand from Brenna's grip. He completely ignored her friend's guidance. "It's going to be okay, sweetie. I'll come back after work and pick you up and make sure you get home okay."

"Baxter, I can take her home," Brenna said. "I get off at three-thirty today too. And I can take her to the hardware store and..."

"Thanks Brenna, but I'd rather her not be alone with those two," Baxter insisted, still holding London tight.

"Baxter, I can..."

"I mean it, London. I don't want you alone with those two. I don't trust them. I'm going with you to the hardware store then taking you home. And I'm going to stay with you tonight just to make sure you're safe."

"Okay. I guess you're not going to take no for an answer," she conceded.

Paranoia prevailed even though London wanted to tell him to back off and that she could take care of herself. If Baxter wanted to protect her, she was going to let him. She realized, however, that there was a very thin line between protection and possession. When the girls sat down later for their afternoon break, Brenna tried to caution her friend about Baxter's tendency to blur that line.

The lunch rush was over. There wasn't a single customer in the place, so Claudia left early. Calvin had gone to the bank. Both cooks were in the kitchen cleaning up. Brenna and London decided to lounge back in the corner booth under the air conditioning vent.

"I could really use a cigarette right now, but it's too freakin' hot out there," Brenna commented.

"You could use a cigarette? How do you think I feel? This has been the craziest day ever. Actually every day has been pretty crazy since Geneva got here. She's making me nuts. I have nightmares every night. And I'm constantly looking over my shoulder feeling like somebody's watching me."

"That deal with your car really freaked you out. Huh?"

"That's putting it mildly," London said, digging in to the order of french fries the girls were sharing. "This whole Brody and Geneva relationship thing gives me the creeps anyway. I understand what she sees in him... Geez, look at him. But why would he want her. She isn't rich yet."

"Are you jealous?"

"I don't want him."

"I know that," Brenna said. She was swirling individual fries in the ketchup and sandwiching them in between her cheeseburger and the upper bun.

"I have never seen anybody eat a cheeseburger and fries that way," London commented, chuckling at her friend's meticulous process.

"Don't change the subject. I asked if you are jealous."

"That's a hard question to answer. I don't think I'm jealous, but seeing them together just reinforces all those feelings and ideas about how he never cared about me in the first place. He was using me the whole time."

"I'm sure he's using her too."

"I know, Brenna. I just... He's making me look bad. And I don't like it."

"Is that why you finally decided to go out with Baxter?"

London anticipated the question at some point, but was dumbfounded by Brenna's timing. There was a long pause before she could answer and even then she was reluctant. Her friend's tone didn't flag that as an innocent, just-out-of-curiosity question.

"That probably had something to do with the timing," she confessed finally. "But I had already kind of made up my mind that I liked him even before that happened. You know that. We talked about it."

"I know. It just seems like things are moving kind of fast."

"Are you talking about us sleeping together? A few hours ago you were ready to throw a party about that."

"I'm talking about the kiss in front of everybody at the diner and..."

"What's wrong with that? I thought it was romantic."

"Exactly," Brenna said. She sat up and turned facing the table. "You hate romance, London. And now all of a sudden you're okay with that? And you're okay with him bossing you around? And me?"

London dropped the fry she was holding and dusted the salt from her hands. "He was trying to look out for me," she insisted. "You were the one encouraging me to admit I had feelings for him."

"I know, Cookie. And I'm glad that you guys are hitting it off so good. He just seems a little bit too emotionally involved in your fight. Know what I mean?" Brenna reached out for her friend's hand.

"A real friend is supposed to be supportive," London charged, scooting across the vinyl seat to leave.

Brenna called out to her as she crossed the dining room. "No. A real friend isn't afraid to tell it like it is. I'm a little worried, London. I love you. I don't want you to get hurt."

London stopped. She was outraged by the accusation, but the sincerity in Brenna's voice compelled her to listen.

"I'm not saying I think Baxter is trying to hurt you on purpose," Brenna explained. "I just don't think he knows a whole lot about boundaries. He seems to really hate Brody and he barely knows the guy."

"Maybe he's good at reading people," London replied.

"Or maybe he's jealous of your past. He's been chasing after you for months and now that he's finally got you in his arms he seems to be holding on a little too tight. That little scene out there by the car today is the perfect example."

"He was insistent. But I think the car thing really freaked him out too."

"We were all freaked out. Believe me," Brenna said. "All I'm saying is have fun with him. Just don't let him take over your life. You've been through so much this past month with losing Grammy. You need time to adjust before you jump into such a serious relationship."

London nodded her head and extended her arms to hug Brenna. She agreed somewhat with her friend's analysis of the situation. Baxter was stubborn and definitely had some strong opinions about her dealings with Geneva. Those feelings were warranted., but she agreed with Brenna's point about his limited knowledge of the big picture. She also felt compelled though to point out that Baxter was privy to things London couldn't see either. He was at that work site everyday watching Geneva tangled in the Wickerford spider web; maybe he knew the answer to whether she was the spider or the prey. That made Baxter a good person to have on her side. Brenna couldn't argue with that point.

Brenna also couldn't argue with London's enthusiasm about the prospect of two weeks with Geneva more than 2000 miles away in California. The hope that she and Brody might not ever return was pointless, but the idea made London almost giddy. She hadn't felt at peace since Geneva's arrival. She looked forward to settling the estate in a few months and finally getting that woman out of her life for good. That seemed like the perfect Christmas present.

Calvin returned from the bank later that afternoon with good news about London's car. He'd talked to Troy at the garage while he was out and learned that the problem was just a bad seal on one of the power steering hoses. That ruled out Geneva's involvement in any foul play with her car. Calvin said very little on the subject, but London read disappointment on his face.

"What's wrong, Calvin? This is good news. Geneva didn't do it," London said.

"I really wish you wouldn't do that."

"Do what?"

"I don't think you realize London how much your grandmother prayed for you and your sister. She loved you both so much," he said. "And she wanted so much for you and Geneva to be close. That's how sisters are supposed to be."

"I know. And I try. Believe me. I try."

"I think you need to try harder, London. This isn't the first time you jumped to the wrong conclusion. Is it?"

London stared at him blankly.

"You don't know I'm listening a lot of the time, but I hear the things you say. What happened to the lessons your grandparents taught you about patience, charity, and forgiveness? You are a better person than that, London."

That was all Calvin said. He gently squeezed her shoulder and walked away. London took his comments to heart. His was one opinion that still mattered. And even he was blaming her for the friction and bitter sibling rivalry. She tried to be conscientious about that when she met Geneva and Brody at the hardware store later that afternoon. His words couldn't magically erase the tension, but the trip was otherwise uneventful.

Assumedly because of Baxter's presence, Brody waited in the car once they got to the house. London stayed out of Geneva's way, except to answer questions about where she'd put Geneva's favorite beach towel and whether or not she could take the afghan from Grammy's rocking chair. Grammy had three afghans, so London had no problem letting Geneva take one. She also knew exactly where to find the beach towel; she remembered laughing at the cute design when she put it in the laundry. The towel had a cartoon picture of a little girl wearing a bathing suit top but no bottoms as she stood in front of a sign that read "no topless sunbathing". She pictured her slutty sister doing the same up at the Wickerford mansion. Geneva thanked London for the afghan, retrieved the towel from the laundry room basket, and left for her great adventures in California. She was in and out within 15 minutes.

After dinner and after discovering that London didn't have cable television for him to watch sports, Baxter switched focus to his only other favorite past time, making love. They were snuggled on the coach. He was kissing her neck and letting his hands wonder up the back of her shirt. London shrugged away from his hungry mouth.

"Don't leave any more marks on my neck there. I don't want to keep having to wear this scarf when it's 100 degrees outside."

"You don't have to hide them," he said, kissing her neck again. "They're a symbol of my love. I'm letting the world know you belong to me."

"I belong to you?" London pushed him away a little more forcefully. Brenna's words were echoing in her head. "I'm your girlfriend. Not your possession."

Baxter grabbed her as she tried to get up from the couch. "Hey! Hey! Where the hell did that come from?" He wasn't angry. He was confused.

" It's just that this is all still so new, Baxter. And you're already talking about love and how I belong to you? You're moving a little too fast for me."

"And you're afraid it's an act," he said.

"I don't know what I'm afraid of," she replied. She turned slightly toward him and stroked the side of his face with her hand. "Maybe I'm just afraid of being too dependent. I watched how my Grammy struggled after my Grampy died. Then I practically fell apart when Brody and I split. I feel like there's a lesson there."

"I know it's hard for you to believe, London, but I do love you. We've only had one date, but I started falling in love with you six months ago when you told me to go play in the trees with the other horny monkeys."

London started laughing, relaxing back on the couch with her hands clasped loosely in front of her mouth. She remembered saying that, but had forgotten all about that day until his reminder. He joined in her laughter.

"You remember that?"

"Yes." She giggled. "I was mad about them cutting down those beautiful trees."

"Yea, but something happened right before I got to the diner. Right? One of those baboon lumberjacks was pawing at you."

"The jerk grabbed my ass and untied my apron every time I walked by. I'm used to that kind of crap. But when he grabbed my boob when I tried to fill the other guy's water glass I had to make Calvin throw him out. I was so pissed off."

Baxter hooked his fingers around hers and rested their intertwined hands down against his leg. "Then I walk in, totally unaware of what had just happened, and I ask you for a date. And you went off the deep end."

"And I screamed at you to go play in the trees with the other monkeys. I remember exactly what I said." London blushed. "I'm sorry about that."

"Don't be sorry. I loved it!" he insisted. "Those first eight months were like foreplay."

"You like it rough?" she teased.

"That's when I realized that tough exterior of yours was nothing more than scar tissue from some pretty deep emotional wounds. And deep beneath those scars was a strong, resilient person with a soft heart." He leaned in, gazed into her eyes, and kissed her softly. "Just like me."

Those words sounded like something out of a romance novel and definitely not something Baxter could come up with on his own, but the sentiment undermined her sense of logic and any lingering resistance to the notion that she was already in love with him too. She kissed him again then led him through the kitchen and down the hall to her bedroom. She closed the door behind them and once again the rest of the world and their opinions had ceased to exist.

Chapter Twelve

A series of short blasts shook the diner and rattled the glassware on the racks in the kitchen. The Mount Karma blasting site was over three miles away. She had heeded Marco's advice about a temporary relocation while they were blasting, but the increasingly loud construction noise when she came back from Brenna's house prompted her to find a more long-term solution. Once the blasting was done, Baxter and his crew were working nightly until six-thirty or seven o'clock. Poor Vienna was frightened all the time. London decided to sign a three month lease at the Cedar Ridge Apartments about ten miles from the diner, just inside the Coral Leaf city limits..

London settled in to her new home and her new relationship rather easily. Baxter moving in was not part of the plan, but he stayed at the apartment most nights. They were in love. For the first time in almost two years London Keller was completely, madly, deeply in love. She learned to deal with the whiskers in the sink and his smelly, muddy work boots by the front door. She'd even done what she could to curb his urge to surprise her with over-the-top romantic gestures. After all, she believed he was the reason her nightmares had stopped and why she'd finally managed to shake that creepy feeling someone was watching her too. She was happy, even after Geneva and Brody returned from California.

For the one month anniversary of their first date, Baxter had arranged for a romantic dinner and double date with Brenna and Seth. Baxter had pulled some strings to get Seth a very good-paying electrician job on the Pine Shadows project. The two guys had become friends. Baxter said he wanted to make peace with Brenna and help resolve her unease about his relationship with

London. Baxter was in love too; he wanted her best friend's blessing.

Baxter left work early that day. He caught London napping on the couch. He startled her awake with a hot, wet kiss on the mouth. Vienna popped out from behind London's knees where she was snoozing and jumped down from the couch.

"Is this what you do all day while I'm at work?" he teased.

She smiled and kissed him again. "I was resting up for tonight. It is our anniversary after all."

"I can't wait for tonight," he said. He kneeled down on the floor in front of the sofa and handed her a hot pink gift box with a thick white ribbon tied into a bow at the top. "I wanted us to be alone when you opened it."

London felt her eyes widen. "What is it?"

"It's a present, silly."

"Baxter, what did you do?" She scooted into a more upright position on the arm of the couch. "I told you I didn't want you to get me any gifts. This is only our one-month anniversary and..."

"Will you just open the box? " he interrupted. "I think you're going to like this."

London pushed her long bangs from her face. She glanced at the box, then at him, and then at the box again as Baxter urged her to take it from his hands. The box was too large for jewelry and too small for any kind of lingerie she'd be willing to wear. She shook her head as she untied the bow and removed the lid. Inside was a smaller box wrapped in heart-covered tissue paper. She peeled back the edges of the tissue to reveal a wooden keepsake box. Framed in the middle of the lid was a glossy ceramic photo tile with a picture of London, Grammy, and Grampy in front of her grandparent's house. This was so unexpected.

"Do you like it?"

"I love it," she whimpered.

Baxter kissed her tenderly and cupped his hands around hers as she held the gift. "I hope you don't mind, but I saw this picture in one of your photo books that last time we spent the night at your grandma's house. I borrowed it the other day when we stopped by to check on things. While you were upstairs."

"It's a beautiful gift, Baxter." London was still overwhelmed by emotion. Her voice was barely a muffle. She glanced at him and smiled. "Who are you?"

Baxter rose from his knees and squeezed onto the edge of the couch facing her. "I'm just the lucky guy about to make love to you." He took the box from her hands and placed it gently on the sofa table behind her head, pressing his body against her and kissing her as he leaned forward. He clutched each of her hands tightly in his and helped her to her feet. His smile was radiant, yet a bit mischievous. "But first we dance."

London protested playfully. "No no no no no no. Don't make me dance. Please. Please."

"Oh yes yes yes."

"So that's why you bought me that gift." London chucked as he scooped her into his arms and began swaying her side to side. "You're trying to bribe me to get me to dance with you."

Baxter kissed her and gazed into her eyes.

"Okay. Fine. But just one."

"And for the rest of our lives," he said.

London couldn't possibly comprehend the hidden meaning in that statement, so she twirled. She twirled like a whimsical fairy with ballet slippers and glittery wings. She shook her booty like a disco dancing queen. And she cut a rug like a girl named Linda Lou until the oven timer dinged. Then she kissed him and declared that the apple pie was done. Saved by the bell from the awkward, tense moment that seemed to be leading to a marriage proposal. She couldn't marry him... Not after only a month.

"You should probably shower and start getting ready," she said. She slipped her hand into an oven mitt and opened the oven door. The crumbles on top of the pie were perfectly browned.

"It's not even three o'clock. Do I smell that bad?"

"No." She laughed. "But we need vanilla ice cream and I want you to go with me to the video store. We're all coming back here after dinner to watch a movie and have dessert." She lifted the pie from the oven rack and set it on the counter to cool.

"Why don't we just have dessert at the restaurant and go see a movie at the theater?"

"I thought you loved Grammy's apple pie."

"I do," he replied, wrapping his arms around her waist. "But I love getting naked with you even more."

"Baxter." She shrugged away from the kiss on her neck.

"And if we skip the trip to the grocery store and the movie place, I can teach you a new kind of dance in the bedroom."

She spun around to face him. "I've heard of that dance you're referring to and I don't want you to rush through my lesson. I am a slow..." She kissed him. "Slow..." She kissed him again. "Slow learner."

Baxter raised his eyebrows and grinned. "Well I hope you don't have to work tomorrow."

London winked, kissed him one more time, then hurried him off to the bedroom for a shower. As soon as she heard the water running, she hurried to call the diner. She couldn't let Baxter know she'd lied about the video; she had to let Brenna know there was a change of plans.

"I had to find some excuse to get us out of the house, so I lied and said we were coming back here after dinner."

"Why all the secrecy? Is everything okay?"

"It's a long story," London replied. "I really need to get off the phone. I swear he showers like it's a drive-through car wash - in and out in 2.5 minutes."

"Should I be worried?"

"No. No. Don't worry. I promise I'll tell you everything. Now I gotta' go. See you at five-thirty."

London hung up the phone before Brenna could ask any more questions. She knew her friend probably ignored the advice about not worrying. In reality, London knew they both should be worried. Baxter was already talking about happily ever after and that was frightening as hell. The only thing that terrified her more was the fact that she was thinking about the same thing. If she hadn't pulled away... If he had asked her to marry him, she would have said yes. Who was this charming, silly-hearted guy singing in her shower? Who was this sentimental fool standing in her kitchen? She recognized her reflection in the window, but had no idea what became of that cynical, untrusting person she once was. So much for resisting his charms. She felt like one of those cartoon characters clinging to the side of a steep mountain, clawing at the dirt as rocks crumbled all around her and fell into the 1000 foot canyon below. That was exactly how she described it to Brenna later that night when they escaped to the ladies room for their highly anticipated private chat.

"Thank God you didn't give him a chance to ask," Brenna said. "You'd have the whole town thinking you're pregnant too."

"I don't care what the town thinks."

"Do you care what I think?"

"Of course I care what you think," London replied. She puckered her lips slightly and drew on some fresh lipstick. "I want to know what you think about this color. Too red?"

"Don't change the subject, London. I was talking about my opinion about Baxter."

London sighed. "I know your opinion about Baxter. That's why I wanted to talk about what he said and all the crazy stuff going through my head. What's happening to me?"

"He has you hypnotized." Brenna chuckled. "I remember when Seth used to make me feel that way."

"How long were you two together before you got married?"

"About a year. I guess we'd been going out for about seven months when he asked me. He proposed on his birthday," she said.

"That's pretty fast too."

"I didn't have a best friend to talk any sense into me."

"Yea, but you're happy. Right?" London dropped the lipstick back into her purse and blotted her lips with a paper towel.

"Most of the time," Brenna replied. "Unless his mother is in town. What about Baxter's family? Do you know anything about them?"

"He doesn't speak to them."

"That doesn't sound good."

"It's a long story," London said. "And we better get back to the table before they send a search party."

"You have to quit doing that to me," Brenna said. She grabbed London's purse strap to stop her from opening the door. "Everything is a long story. You used to love telling me long stories. You're always so worried about what Baxter is gonna' say or what Baxter is gonna' think. I'm sick of it. This guy is taking over your life."

"This doesn't have anything to do with you," she scowled. "I know he's taking over my life. That's what I've been saying. I am head over heels, totally out of control and I am scared to death. I want to break up with him because he's moving too fast, but then I can't stand the thought of a single moment without him."

Brenna leaned back against the bathroom vanity and folded her arms.

"I'm sorry if that makes you mad. I know you don't trust him..."

"I never said I don't trust him," Brenna interrupted. "I like Baxter. It just freaks me out to see you so absorbed in this relationship. And I know this is going to piss you off, but I have to say it. I'm worried that this is a rebound thing."

"Rebound?" London squawked. "Brody and I broke up almost 2 years ago."

"But you spent those two years taking care of your sick grandmother. This is you time. This is London time. Not get-even-with-Geneva-for-stealing-your-ex-boyfriend time. Brody Danbrook is not worth throwing away your whole life."

"That is not what this is," she insisted.

"Maybe you're not doing it intentionally, but it's gotta' be killing you inside that she is with him now and having his baby. My heart broke for you that day. I couldn't sleep that night. Then a couple days later you came into work and you were suddenly in a relationship with Baxter."

London shook her head. "Why is this coming up now?

"This is what I've been trying to tell you all along. And why I was too busy to help you move into the apartment. And why I've been so distant," Brenna said.

"Baxter thinks you hate him."

"I know. Seth told me. That's why I agreed to this dinner, which is probably out there at the table getting cold about now."

"We should get back," London agreed.

"I'll be especially nice to Baxter tonight so he knows I don't hate him. You just promise me you're not going to..." Brenna paused. "Never mind. It's your decision. Just be careful with those rainbows and sunshine flying out of your ass."

London laughed and hugged her friend. "I love you."

"I love you too, Cookie."

London pushed open the ladies room door. She re-entered the restaurant dining area determined to heed Brenna's advice and resist Baxter's magical spell, but that determination faded almost the instant she saw his smiling face. She was thrilled to watch him interact with her friends, asking questions about Brenna's kids and laughing at Seth's corny jokes. She liked the way he enjoyed her homemade apple pie and shared her taste in movies. Most of all she loved the butterfly-in-a-whirlwind emotion she felt when Baxter touched her and loved her so passionately through the late night hours. She wanted to marry this man, but alas morning came without the proposal she desired.

Baxter rose early and went to work as usual. London slept in for another hour then spent the morning with a hot cup of tea and a book by her favorite author, Drake Roberts. The book was about the author and the love of his life – a relationship that started out as a teenage crush. London had multiple crushes as a teenager and she remembered the stories Grammy told every time some jerk broke her heart. Over and over, Vera assured her granddaughter that true love really existed. Suddenly, as if Grammy's spirit was guiding her, she revisited that frightening cartoon image from the previous day. Perhaps she wasn't clawing the side of the mountain to keep from falling. Maybe she was climbing that mountain instead. Perhaps Baxter was waiting for her at the top of that mountain and she was digging and clawing her way to the top as fast as she could. Perhaps London was finally ready to let go of her past and the darkness that cast a shadow in the deep canyon below.

Letting go of the past also meant finally saying goodbye and embracing a future without Grammy by her side. London withdrew from the comfort of her living room arm chair and retreated to the walk-in closet in her bedroom. There, still tucked in the zipper compartment of her little black purse, was her grandmother's final farewell – the letter Nurse Wendy penned for her on the cherished pink stationary.

> I'm sad to say goodbye to you, London, but please know that I'm ready and that I am at peace with God's will. Nothing in life prepares you for losing someone you love and nothing can ever take that person's place in your heart, but life does go on somehow. Some way. And sometimes the loveliest gifts are the ones you least expect at the times you least expect them. I hope you are

happy with the life your Grampy and I made for you. I hope our love is enough to carry you through these difficult days and weeks ahead. Like your love helped me through.

I am so proud of you, London. And I'm so proud to be your grandmother. Whatever happens and wherever life's road leads you after I'm gone, promise me that you'll remember the importance of family. I will always be with you in spirit and in love. Don't forget to let others in too once in a while to help protect you.

Thank you so much for making my life so, so beautiful. I love you.

London read the letter a second time before replacing it in the envelope. She *was* happy with the life her grandparents made for her. The only thing she wished for was more time and more answers.

Grammy's words were kind and beautiful, and the letter definitely provided closure, but all of the things in that letter were things her grandmother expressed often. The letter contained the advice London expected about opening her heart, but she was no closer to an answer about Baxter. She talked about the importance of family, but there was no mention of her house or the estate. There were also no hints about her father's identity. London felt certain she knew the answer and though she'd asked many times through the years, Grammy refused to say. She had hoped for confirmation finally. Either Grammy truly didn't know or she preferred to keep that a mystery forever.

Chapter Thirteen

The clouds drooped dark and heavy with rain and sank low toward the Coral Leaf skyline. London watched through her kitchen window as the weather moved in from the northwest. The jagged, tree-lined mountain peaks seemed to puncture the clouds as the wind pushed them across the sky and the rain started falling hard and steady. The rain was a welcomed sight after weeks of drought and summer heat and the perfect excuse to stay home from work and take care of her boyfriend. Baxter was home for a second day with a severe case of poison ivy on his hands and neck. He had just returned from the doctor's office. London was making him lunch.

London's kitchen overlooked the parking lot behind her apartment building. From the window above the sink, she saw Calvin pull into the lot and jump out of his car with a sense of urgency. Before she could contemplate the possible reason for his visit, he was knocking at the door... Actually pounding at the door. She answered the door in a panic. Calvin was there. Another long-time family friend, Sheriff Harrison Dodd, was on his way up the front steps too.

"What's the matter? What is it?" She remembered a scene like this from her childhood. The night her mother died. In fact, Harrison's older brother Gene was the one to notify Vera and Montgomery that their daughter had been killed. Reverend Walker was with him that night too.

"It's your sister," Calvin said. "She was attacked. She's in the hospital."

London gasped. "Oh my God. Is she okay?"

The sheriff cleared his throat then asked if he could step inside..

"Harrison, you are scaring me. Why are you both here?" London begged. Calvin looked frightened and pale. She gestured for them to come inside, but stayed close to the door. "Is she um... Dead?"

"Your sister survived the attack, London. But we're not sure about the baby. She was bleeding pretty severely."

"Who would do such a thing?"

"That's why I'm here, London."

"What does this have to do with me? Geneva and I barely speak. We hate each..."

London didn't finish the sentence. Suddenly she realized she might be a suspect. Her quarrel with Geneva was quite public and so was her rumored resentment about Geneva's pregnancy and her ^relationship with Brody. She looked down at her feet, debating about whether or not to call out for Baxter. Would he become a suspect too?

Harrison placed his hand on London's shoulder, clearly sensing her frantic state of mind. "She said it was Seth Reese."

London looked up abruptly and shook her head. Harrison's hand slipped from her shoulder as she backed away from him. "What? That's impossible. Seth is... Brenna is my... They are happily married and..."

"We're investigating, London."

She called out for Baxter as the sheriff continued.

" I wasn't there. The emergency operator dispatched the Conners Bluff PD. They took Seth into custody."

"Brenna is there with him now," Calvin added. "She asked me to come for you."

"I can't believe this," London said, wrenching her hands nervously.

Baxter emerged from the bedroom, puzzled by the commotion. "Are you okay? What's happened?"

Harrison interjected before London could explain the situation. His facial expression shifted. "Sick day today, Baxter?"

"Bad case of poison ivy," Baxter answered.

"Have you been here all morning?" Harrison asked.

"What's going on here?"

"Evie Charles was attacked this morning at the Wickerford house."

London stepped between the sheriff and Baxter. "She said Brenna's husband did it."

"That doesn't make any sense. Seth Reese wouldn't hurt anybody," Baxter insisted.

"Seth was the one who called the ambulance. He told the other officers that he heard her crying and found her there inside."

"So you don't think he did it either," Baxter said, putting his arm around London's shoulder.

"We're not ruling anything out," the sheriff replied coldly. "What time did you leave work yesterday?"

London started walking back toward the sheriff. Harrison didn't move and his eyes remained focused on Baxter.

"He was…" London said.

Harrison held up his hand to silence her and presumably stop her from getting any closer. "I'm just asking some questions here. Nobody needs to get defensive."

"I was sick yesterday," Baxter said.

"You look a lot different without the beard and all the hair. When did you do that?" Harrison asked. Judgment and scrutiny crimped the corners of the sheriff's mouth and hardened his jaw line.

Baxter folded his arms across his chest. "What difference does that make?"

"I just wonder why you'd make such a drastic change to your appearance."

"I just wonder why that's any of your damn business."

"Listen here, pal…"

London interrupted the conversation, nervous that Baxter's attitude was making him seem guilty. There was no way he was involved. "Harrison, why are you asking all these questions? He didn't do this."

"I didn't say he did this," Harrison said. "I'm just trying to get to the bottom of what happened here. We might have an innocent man locked up at the moment and I'd like to get him home to his wife and children."

Baxter stepped between London and the sheriff and nudged her aside. "It's okay, London. I'll answer his questions."

London tried again to shift the focus away from her boyfriend. "Can't this wait, Harrison? Baxter was with me here all night and all morning. Brenna needs me."

"The poor girl is a wreck," Calvin added. "Can't we just..."

Harrison continued questioning Baxter without regard for their comments. "You didn't go anywhere? I checked your truck. The hood is still warm."

"Of course it's warm. It's 90 degrees outside," London argued.

"I went to the doctor at eight-thirty. He gave me a shot of prednisone."

"But London I thought you said he was here with you all morning. Why..."

A woman's voice crackled through Harrison's radio and cut off his sentence. He withdrew the radio from his belt loop and stepped outside the front door to respond .

"London, you're going to get yourself into a lot of trouble here," Calvin warned. "You shouldn't be lying."

"He's right," Baxter said. "I don't need you to lie for me. I don't have anything to hide. Neither do you."

London leaned in and whispered. "I think he thinks you did it."

"He's just doing his job, babe. They try to trip you up so they can tell whether you're telling the truth or not. You lying isn't going to help."

"I just don't want to..."

Harrison stepped back in through the front door. "Well, that was Deputy Manning. She's at the hospital. Geneva's accusation was a misunderstanding."

"They made a mistake?" London was relieved, but angered. "They arrested an innocent man because of a misunderstanding?"

"She was confused. She lost a lot of blood and was fading in and out of consciousness. She was trying to tell them that Seth saved her life. It didn't come out that way apparently," Harrison replied. "They've already released your friend's husband. There were never any actual charges filed."

"I have to get over there to Brenna's."

"You're not going to go to the hospital?" Calvin asked. "Your sister needs you."

London looked up at the reverend. She was already sitting on the ottoman putting her shoes on. "I'm not sure she'd want to see me."

"You are family," he replied firmly. "Come on, you can ride to the hospital with me."

She didn't know how to tell him no.

Geneva was sitting up in bed when they arrived at the hospital. She was conscious and alert, talking to Alma-Rae and the nurse tending to her IV. She had a large bandage around her head with some blood seepage in the front from an obvious wound on her forehead. Her chin was stitched up and she also appeared to have a few broken teeth in the front.

Calvin greeted Geneva and Alma-Rae and offered his sympathy. "I came as soon as I heard, Evie. I'm so very sorry for your loss."

Even Calvin was calling her Evie? As far as London knew, they'd met only once at Grammy's memorial service.

"I want you to know if there's anything I can do..."

"Thank you, Reverend. But I am going to be okay," Geneva said, reaching for his hand. "I know the baby is with her grandma and great grandma now."

London wanted to throw up. She felt genuine sympathy and concern for Geneva's situation, but could barely refrain from calling bullshit. Geneva was exploiting Grammy's memory for her own benefit and everyone in the room was falling for it. Alma-Rae's overly dramatic response only made matters worse.

"That's right." Alma-Rae teared up and hugged Geneva. "That blessed baby is surrounded by love right now. We know that for sure."

Calvin squeezed Geneva's hand. "I'll pray for you and your family."

London sat down on the edge of the armchair in the corner of the room. Geneva had looked at her, but not yet acknowledged her presence in the room. She cleared her throat and sought words to hide her disgust with her carrying on. "What did the doctor say?"

Geneva cringed. "What do you care? What are you even doing here?"

"I was concerned."

"She came with me," Calvin added. "Sisters care about one another."

"She doesn't care about me," Geneva argued. "You don't have to worry, London. I already told the cops they made a mistake when they arrested Seth. I have a concussion. And I was scared and bleeding a lot from my head and all confused. And they put that damn oxygen thing over my mouth so I couldn't tell them what happened. The police saw me bleeding down there and just assumed."

"The sheriff already told us that."

Alma-Rae gently caressed Geneva's hand. "I hadn't gotten home yet from my weekend at Harlan's place. She said she started bleeding really bad and was trying to get to the phone to call for help. She hit my head and... Well, Seth called 9-1-1."

"Where is Brody?" Calvin asked. "How is handling this?"

"He's on his way home," Alma-Rae said. "He went down to Florida with me to look for a rental property for this winter. I wanted them to come down there this year with me for the Christmas season."

"Don't tell her all that," Geneva demanded. "It's none of her business."

"Geneva, I know we've had our differences, but I am very sorry about the baby."

"No you're not," she grunted.

Alma-Rae squeezed her hand. "Evie, don't talk like that."

"You probably think I deserve this," Geneva continued. "Like I'm some kind of evil person or something. I heard the things you said to Brody about me. And all the other things you've been saying all over town about me. I'm not stupid."

London got up from the chair and responded calmly. "I didn't come here to fight with you. I'm really sorry that this happened to you."

"Just get out," Geneva demanded.

London didn't respond. She left the room as Geneva asked and took a seat in the waiting room while Calvin finished paying his respects. The thought that Geneva deserved this had never once crossed her mind, but she understood the emotion that led to the statement. She hadn't been a good sister. Despite all her grandparents taught her, London was – for those first months of their relationship – a bad sister. She was bitter and selfish, and completely incapable of accepting the fact that somebody else loved Grammy. Did she trust her? No. Did she want to be close with Geneva? No, but she wanted to be a better person. She wanted to honor the importance of family and her Grammy's wishes.

Baxter joined London later that afternoon as she headed out to Whispering Trails to check on Brenna. Seth was obviously thankful for his release. The kids swarmed around their father, frightened and unwilling to leave his side. Brenna was furious.

"Now your sister is ruining everyone else's life too," Brenna fumed. She paced angrily in front of the television.

"I'm so sorry," London said.

"It was a misunderstanding, honey. I'm home. No charges. Everything is fine," Seth said.

Brenna looked down at her children. "Libby, take your brother into the bedroom and play."

"But mommy..."

"Now, Libby. The grown-ups need to talk."

Libby got up from the couch and reluctantly carried her little brother down the hall. Tyler was kicking and screaming. He wanted his daddy.

"The sheriff said..."

Brenna interrupted Baxter as he started to recount what Harrison had told them at the apartment. "I don't care what the sheriff said. People aren't going to care that the charges were dropped. All they're going to talk about is the fact that my loving husband was arrested for attacking that little whore."

"Honey, calm down," Seth urged.

London sat down on one of the kitchen chairs, noting the sarcasm in her use of the word "loving". Baxter stood next to her and placed his hand on her shoulder.

"I can't calm down." Brenna turned slightly and stared right at London. "Some of this is your fault. If you weren't so stubborn about selling your grandmother's house, that bitch would be gone and none of this would have happened."

"Hey!" Baxter charged.

"You're blaming me?"

Brenna continued rambling, uninterested in either response. "You're all high and mighty talking about how much you love

Grammy and how terrible it is that the Wickerfords want to buy her house and how Geneva is just a traitor sucking up to them.... All while you're screwing *him*." Brenna pointed angrily at Baxter then looked down at the floor. "You don't even live there anymore for crying out loud. Why can't you just sell that damn place and send her on her way?"

London stood up and walked toward the door. She didn't look back at her. She didn't say a word. As she reached the door and wrapped her fingers around the handle, Brenna returned her focus to her husband. Finally, the real source of her friend's frustration was revealed.

"What I want to know is what the fuck were you doing in that house anyway? Are you sleeping with her too?"

Seth threw his hands up in the air. "Here we go again. I'm not cheating on you, Brenna!"

Baxter placed his hand in the small of London's back and urged her to continue out the front door. He led her down the front porch steps and to the car. She sensed that he knew something. Curiosity had her senses tingling. Brenna didn't deserve a cheating husband, but she was intrigued by the possibility that Geneva was cheating on her fiancé. Brody did deserve that after the hell he put her through.

London got into the car and immediately started asking questions. Her desire to be a better person had apparently gotten into the back seat. "Do you know something you're not telling me?"

"There's a fireworks show about to happen," he said, starting the car.

"Is he sleeping with Geneva?"

"I don't know about Geneva," he said. "But Marco said he saw him with the housekeeper Sharla the other day."

"Why didn't you tell me that?"

"Because I didn't see anything. And because I'm not gonna' be the one to break up the guy's marriage. Your best friend doesn't need another reason to hate me."

"Well, she's not my best friend anymore," London said. "I can't believe she actually blamed me for all this. She knows how much that house means to me. How could she ask me to sell it?"

Baxter turned on the windshield wipers to clear away the light, speckled mist. "She does have a point though, London."

London looked at him over her shoulder. "What are you saying?"

"You aren't living there. You've got the nice apartment now and..."

"You're the one who told me to get the apartment," she argued. "And you know it's just temporary until the construction is over."

"London, look at how happy you've been since you moved out of that dark, claustrophobic little valley."

"That has nothing to do with Grammy's house."

"You told me yourself that you're sleeping better and that you haven't had a bad dream since you moved out. Maybe it was that house. Maybe your grandparents' spirits were..."

"I do not believe in ghosts," London demanded. "And I can't believe you're saying this to me."

"Baby, I'm not trying to upset you."

"Do not call me baby."

"London, please."

She didn't respond. She turned her head back forward and stared through the windshield. Baxter stopped the car.

"I'm trying to have a conversation with you."

"Put the car back in drive and take me home," she demanded. "I don't want to fight with you."

Baxter leaned over the armrest and center console. He talked softly and calmly into her ear. "You're mad at me, but we're not fighting. All I'm saying is that Brenna has a point about Geneva making you crazy."

A tear trickled from the corner of her eye. She tried to wipe it away quickly without him noticing. "I cannot sell Grammy's house. That land belongs to my family. I can't just give it away."

"Okay. I'm sorry I upset you, baby. I didn't mean to make you cry."

"Please just take me home. I'm tired."

Chapter Fourteen

Days passed without a word between London and Brenna. She even quit her job at the diner so they wouldn't have to face each other. This wasn't the first time a man had caused friction between her and a friend, but this was the first time London took the man's side. No matter what emotional crisis Brenna was going through, London refused to be friends with someone who considered her a hypocrite. After two years and countless conversations about her grandmother, Brenna should have known better than to make a statement like that. She'd confided in Brenna about her fears of losing the most important person in her life. She trusted her with secrets after she and Brody broke up – secrets she never shared with anyone else, not even Grammy. Brenna was also one of the people who inspired London to open her heart to the possibility of falling in love again. Her criticism felt like betrayal.

Brenna's commentary on the subject of Baxter did help London though; her doubts about their relationship were finally alleviated. Tensions still remained high between the couple, but she didn't completely cut off communication with him. They just slept apart for the next few days. He slept on the couch the first night. London returned to her Grammy's house without him the next morning. She told Baxter she needed time alone to think. He didn't argue.

London found comfort again in the familiar surroundings, with all the family photos and her childhood memories. Vienna found comfort in resuming her position in bed, curled up beneath the blankets in the small of her momma's back. The early morning construction noise was annoying, but they still both managed to embrace the sleep-til-noon concept. The nightmares stayed away too. Unfortunately Geneva didn't.

Geneva roused her and the dog from bed just after eight o'clock on the third morning. London had closed her bedroom door the night before out of habit, but she would have needed tranquilizers to sleep through the racket her sister was making in the living room. Over the top of Vienna's bewildered barking, London could hear male voices too. What the hell was going on? She grabbed her robe and charged into the kitchen. Geneva was sitting at the table drinking coffee.

"What are you doing?"

"I'm drinking coffee, silly. What does it look like I'm doing?" Geneva gestured at the Starbucks logo on the side of her cup. "That's one good thing about not being pregnant anymore. I can have caffeine again."

London rolled her eyes and replied sarcastically. "Oh gee. I'm happy for you then."

"I knew you'd say something ignorant. That's just how you are."

"Whatever. What are you doing here drinking coffee?" London glanced into the living room. The front door was open and two tall, bodybuilder-type guys were entering the living room. Theirs were obviously the male voices she heard. "And who the hell are those guys?"

"That's Sam and Big Tommy. They're helping me move some stuff."

London started into the living room. The china cabinet and dining room set were gone, her mother's painting had been moved from above the fireplace, and Grammy's wheelchair was missing. "Where is Grammy's chair?"

"I got rid of it."

"Get it back. You had no right to get rid of that chair."

"Why would you want to keep a stupid wheelchair? Grammy hated that thing. She told me every day about how she felt like a prisoner. She missed her long walks with her dog. And dancing with Grandpa. She wanted to be free. And now she is," Geneva said. "Why would you want to hang on to that?"

London didn't have an answer. She turned and disappeared back into her bedroom without saying anything further. She had no idea why she had such a sentimental attachment to it. Grammy's empty wheelchair was always the first thing London noticed when she walked through the door and it represented the void she felt in her heart since Vera's passing. She felt ashamed for forgetting how much her grandmother hated that chair and even more that Geneva was the one to remind her. Her Grammy was finally free. She was no longer blind and helpless, and her pain was finally gone.

Geneva followed London through the kitchen and stood in her bedroom doorway. "Grammy would hate to see you like this. I think she'd want us to live happy. There's a whole bunch of world to see out there on the other side of these mountains. You don't even know what you're missing."

London rubbed the tears from her eyes. "Okay, stop. You made your point."

"Keepin' Grammy's house ain't gonna' bring her back."

"I said stop it. I'm not selling! Now, get the hell out of my room."

"Whatever. I tried," Geneva said. She turned around and started exiting the room. "If you ain't gonna sell then I'm just gonna' take my stuff."

"Oh no you're not," London insisted, following Geneva back into the main living room. The guys were starting to wrap blankets around Grammy's piano. She became frantic and began yelling at the guys. "Get your filthy hands off my stuff! That's my piano. Grammy wanted me to have it."

"Do you even know how to play?" Geneva taunted, gesturing for the movers to continue with their work.

"That's not the point."

Geneva crossed in front of London and sat down casually on the arm of the sofa. She stared at her with a spiteful expression on her face. "Okay, let's talk about the point. Let's talk about how you're trying to keep all this stuff for yourself."

London didn't say anything. Big Tommy was moving the picture frames and trinkets from the top of the piano. She grabbed them from his hands and tried forcing him and Sam to stop.

"I talked to a lawyer, London. A good one. He said that the reason the estate isn't settled yet is because you contested the will or something like that. You're trying to take everything by saying that Grammy was crazy, out of her mind to add me to her will."

"I didn't say she was crazy. Her mental capacity was already challenged before you even contacted her. She wasn't in her right mind to be making such a decision."

"Well, you're not going to win. All I have to do is tell them about the bank account you hid from me," Geneva threatened.

London tugged at the blankets the movers were trying to wrap around the piano. She didn't respond to Geneva's accusation.

"We did some digging and it turns out that fancy little apartment you're shacking up in is being paid for with money from *my* Grammy's checking account."

"My name is on that account."

"But it's my money too. Half of it. My lawyer says you owe me $16,742. You and your boyfriend are using up the money pretty fast, so I decided just to take stuff instead."

"You can't do this."

"Try and stop me," Geneva challenged. She set her coffee cup down on the fireplace mantle. "You think I've caused you trouble before, you just try and stop me from taking what's mine. Everybody knows you hate me. Everybody knows you have a bad temper. I'll give Sam over there a nice blow job to rough me up a little bit and say you did it."

"You are sick."

"And they'd believe me." Geneva kept going, completely unphased by London's words or hateful facial expressions. "Sometimes it pays to be a stupid little whore. Alma-Rae is practically in love with me. Brody didn't even know what hit him."

"Were you ever really even pregnant?"

"Yea, but I doubt it was his. I doubt it was Denny Chapman's evil spawn either. I only slept with him the once to get to Alma-Rae." Geneva chuckled. "See all that time under the bleachers really paid off for me. I learned so much about how to get what I want."

"People will eventually see you for who you really are, Geneva."

"Like your friend Brenna? I talked to her. She showed up at the house two days ago and accused me of sleeping with her husband."

"I'm surprised she didn't fucking strangle you."

"Oh, I think she wanted to... At first. But then I told her about how much I loved Brody and how broken hearted I was that he dumped me when I lost the baby."

"You and Brody broke up?" London asked coldly.

"Yep. And Brenna and I ended up comforting each other all night long. Did you know she was into a little girl-on-girl action? She's a very sexually frustrated woman. She even taught me a couple of things."

"Stop with the fucking lies!" London wanted to hit her, punch her, or slam her to the ground, but then she'd have to take out the two bulky neaderthal bodyguards. Her head was spinning in a dizzy fury.

"And it's a shame too. I think that little piece of knowledge might have saved her marriage."

"Get out of this house. Now! Get out."

"Or what? You gonna' call the cops?" Geneva laughed again. "I already fucked the sheriff too. On my first day in town. I let him do me in the back of his squad car when he tried to give me a ticket for speeding. He didn't even know who I was."

"I don't believe you." London folded her arms and leaned back against the wall. Ugly hatred stirred in her stomach. She felt like she was going to get sick.

Geneva laughed, seemingly amused by the predicament she'd created for London. "How long do you think it's been since the reverend banged his frigid wife?"

"That's it. Get out! Get out of this house!" The blood vessels burst in London's right eye from the force of her scream. The white of her eye immediately changed color as though someone had slashed it with a thick red marker. London didn't see the damage until Geneva and the neanderthals departed, but one look in the mirror revealed why her sister referred to her as "scary devil eye" on her way out the door.

When London failed all attempts to disregard Geneva's trash talk, she resorted to a nap. Unfortunately, the drama in her living room that morning was enough to influence her self-conscience and inspire her first nightmare in weeks. In the beginning of the dream she was dressed in a long, luxurious evening gown with diamonds sparkling around her neck and on her ring finger. Her escort wasn't Baxter, but he also wasn't anyone she recognized. As she danced with the stranger beneath an elegant crystal chandelier, she somehow became aware that she was at the grand opening of the Pine Shadows Resort hotel. She spun around, enjoying the magnificent landscape through the floor-to-ceiling windows, but with each spin the identity of her dance partner started to change: first Brody, then Alma-Rae, then Hadley, then Harrison Dodd, then Baxter, and finally Geneva. As London pulled away, Geneva dug her fingernails deep into the flesh on her arm. London felt no pain, but blood started dripping down the length of her fingers and onto the floor. Drop after drop the pool of blood grew wider and deeper. She was all alone in the middle of the dance floor by this point and she was scared to death.

Horrific images flashed before London's eyes, reflected in the pool of blood at her feet. She saw Grammy suffocated with a pillow. She saw Brenna strangled from behind with a telephone cord as she stood primping in front of the mirror. Hadley shot Denny in the head then jumped from the top of the mountainside hotel. She awakened in her grandmother's bedroom just before seeing him fall to his death. Still in the midst of her nightmare, London moved to the bedroom window.

Night was falling and only a narrow band of sunlight still reflected on Lake Amethyst. She spotted a curious-looking bird soaring above the lavender-shaded water. He was moving in her direction toward the house. The bird's silhouette grew wider and wider as his speed increased and his intent became more clear. Once face to face she realized that curious-looking bird was actually a malicious dragon. A puff of smoke billowed from his nostrils and fire erupted from the dragon's angry jowls. The flames ignited the curtains and all the bedroom furnishings around her. The room was fully engulfed, but she remained untouched. The dragon grunted and she heard a woman cry out. This woman was Geneva, but she wasn't in any pain. She was getting fucked on Grammy's bed by her mystery dance partner. London stumbled backward in horror and tripped over her own body crumpled lifelessly on the floor in a pool of blood.

The nightmare rattled London. She wasn't sure if her life was really in danger, but she wasn't sticking around that house to find out. In fact, she wanted to get as far away from West Virginia as possible. She couldn't warn the others as they'd think she was crazy, but she wasn't leaving without Baxter. Fortunately, he was easy to convince and he knew the perfect place for their escape. Marco had talked once at the diner about his rental property on Casalon Beach in South Carolina. Apparently he had also extended an invitation for Baxter to stay at the beachside condo any time.

London had never been anywhere besides the mountains of West Virginia. Her first visit to the ocean was just the distraction she needed.

Marco and his wife, Anna-Mary, lived about twenty miles inland in a small community named Jessamine Gardens. The couple welcomed London and Baxter during the first night of their visit, then drove them out to Casalon Beach the next day and helped them get setup in the condo. Anna-Mary helped London stock the refrigerator and pantry while Marco showed Baxter around the marina across the street. He also showed off his brand new sailboat he named The Shark Fin. Marco was headed back to Coral Leaf later that day, but promised the two couples would go sailing together on the upcoming weekend when he returned.

Chapter Fifteen

Candlelight dinners. Walking hand-in-hand on the beach at sunrise. Bubble baths for two. Making love with the warm ocean breeze blowing in through open windows. Casalon Beach was paradise for Baxter's romantic side and London didn't seem to mind. She surrendered to the ocean's charm and artistic beauty, and embraced the waves of emotion that washed over her with every kiss, every starry gaze, and every stroke of her hair. She never wanted to leave his arms.

"We should stay here forever," London said.

"In bed?"

She kissed him and rested her head against his chest. "Here in paradise."

"I would love that too, but I don't think Marco will just let us stay here forever."

"I know."

Baxter kissed the top of her head and squeezed her tightly.

"I made a decision though."

"What's that?"

"I'm going to sell my Grammy's property to the Wickerfords." The words burned like acid passing across her lips, but London had made up her mind.

Baxter lifted himself up into a seated position, forcing London to move as well. He gazed at her curiously with his back against the pillows. "Are you sure? What made you change your mind?"

"Geneva is never going to let us be happy. She is never going to rest until I sell that house," London said. "I was so wrapped up in not letting her win. I didn't realize that she was winning anyway by making me miserable."

Baxter tilted his head.

"This is how I want to feel all the time. Happy and safe."

"And satisfied," he joked.

London stretched up to kiss him. "I love you. I mean I am so in love with you, Baxter. I can't.... And I know we've only..."

"Marry me," he said, interrupting her mindless rambling.

Baxter grabbed her hand and placed it with his against his heart. London stared into his deep, soulful blue eyes. There was passion, there was love, and there were tears.

"Let's make each other happy, safe, and satisfied for the rest of our lives," he said.

"Okay," she whimpered.

"Okay? Okay?" Excitement beamed from his smile.

London chuckled as he wrestled her onto her back and climbed on top of her. "Yes. Yes. I will marry you."

"Yes! Yes!" He screamed.

Baxter slipped his fingers between hers and slid her arms up over her head. He forced his mouth against hers for a kiss like she had never felt. Her heart raced to catch his rhythm. Her engine roared like a 747 jet airplane as his face disappeared beneath the sheets and down between her thighs. He had never tried harder to please her. She had never tried harder to make it last. She couldn't tell exactly what he was doing with this fingers, his lips, or his tongue, but every nerve and every fiber in her body was tingling. If he was trying to keep her from changing her mind, he... Never mind. Her eyes were rolling back in her head by this time. She was done thinking about everything.

London Ellayna Keller and Baxter Kenneth Bruce were married three days later in an at-sea wedding aboard Marco's boat. Anna-Mary's cousin was an ordained minister; he performed the ceremony with Anna-Mary and Marco as witnesses. This was the happiest day of London's life. She never even thought this amount of happiness was possible. She also never thought it was possible to have so much sex. They were at sea. Marco and his wife were taking care of Vienna. There really wasn't much else to do besides enjoy each other. Brenna would have called London a freak. London kind of missed that.

Arriving at the agonizing decision to sell the Keller family property was difficult. Actually calling her lawyer to set those wheels in motion was the hardest thing London had done. She'd purposely waited until after the wedding and after their two day honeymoon sail, but right before she and Baxter began their journey back to Coral Leaf. The lawyer questioned London extensively about her change of heart, almost implying at times he suspected she was making her decision under duress.

"Nobody is holding a gun to my head," she assured him. "This is the only way I'll ever have any peace. The only way I can get my sister out of my life."

"Okay, Miss Keller. I will begin processing the paperwork to send over to the Wickerford's legal team," he said. "Stop by my office when you get back into town and we'll discuss next actions."

London felt in that moment like she was saying goodbye again to her Grammy and Grampy, and she cried tears for the sadness she knew they'd feel if they were looking down and watching her actions. She wished in that moment, just like she had 27 years earlier when her mother died, that her sister had never been born at all. This was probably the worst day of her life. Baxter was supportive.

"You made the right decision," Baxter said, trying to comfort her as she hung up the telephone. "I know you're hurting right now, but maybe now you can finally move on."

"I am ready to move on," she said. "I'm ready to start my happily-ever-after with you."

Baxter hugged his new bride and whispered that he loved her. She clung to him and begged him to never let go. He promised.

Within 24 hours the Wickerford's lawyers had responded to London's offer. She got the call just after breakfast. They agreed to buy the Keller property for 2.3 million dollars, stipulating their willingness to pay a $200,000 bonus if she vacated within 10 days. Geneva agreed immediately the 10 day closing period. London was reluctant to accept. Once again, Baxter tried to be supportive.

"Ten days? Baxter, my whole life is in that place. I've lived there since I was five years old. My mother grew up in that place. How can I just let go so fast?"

"Is it going to be any easier to let go in 30 days? Or 60 days?"

"No. I guess not. But at least I would have time to get used to the idea. My life is changing so fast. Six weeks ago I was ready to burn the place down before I let anyone else have it. And I was hoping you'd finally take the hint and leave me alone. And now we're married." London paused, shocked to hear those words come out of her mouth.

"Are you okay?"

"We're freakin' married," she exclaimed. She clasped her hands in front of her mouth and shook her head.

"Stop. Stop. Stop. Stop," he said.

"I don't think I can go through with this."

"Don't start having second thoughts on me now. Please." He wrapped his arms around her and pulled her close. He stared down at her. His blue eyes glistened with a teary haze. "We're already married, baby. We love each other. Remember? That's all that matters. It doesn't matter where we live or whether we have money. Our love is all that matters."

"I have to get out of here for a little bit. I need to go for a walk," she said.

"London…"

"I'm okay, Baxter. I promise. I just need to be by myself for a little bit. Then we'll go get Vienna and start heading home."

London stood along the shoreline just close enough for the shallow surf to reach her bare toes. Her fragile state of mind had just as much to do with positive change as it did with fear. Baxter had introduced her to a whole new world – one she never would have seen from deep in the valleys of Coral Leaf. She looked out at the edgeless stretch of water and recited her grandmother's best advice aloud to herself. "When mistakes of your past cast no shadow on your future decisions, you've been left in the dark." This *was* different. Baxter was different and she had learned from her mistakes with Brody. She wasn't in the dark.

The scenery and soothing rhythm of the ocean waves helped calm London. In her heart, she believed this was the happiness Grammy wanted for her. London's cell phone started ringing as she stood there. It was a fancy new smart phone Baxter had bought for her; he'd changed the ringtone to a song titled *Angels and Heroes*. Perhaps someone thought she needed a sign. Her lawyer was already calling back to let her know that the Wickerford's lawyer had completed his formal review of the contract. The attorney also extended best wishes to the newlyweds on behalf of Alma-Rae and the family. News of their wedding had made it back to Coral Leaf before they did.

Mrs. London Bruce returned to Coral Leaf with 10 days to vacate her childhood home. That meant spending every waking hour at the house packing and down-sizing. She planned to extend the lease on her apartment for another three months so that she and Baxter could take their time deciding their next move. Reliving the memories was painful. Doing all of this without her best friend was miserable. Seth had left town, according to Baxter, and filed for divorce. She wondered how Brenna was handling that situation without her best friend too.

Brenna finally called on closing day. The girls hadn't spoken in almost three weeks. Brenna didn't really apologize. Neither did London, but their mutual resentment seemed to have subsided... at least from what she could tell over the phone.

"I heard you got married," Brenna said. "Congratulations."

"Do you mean that?"

"Yes. I do."

"I wish you could have been there," London said. "It wasn't the same without you."

"You could have called."

"I didn't think you'd approve."

There was silence on the other end for a moment.

"Are you still there, Brenna?"

"I'm still here. I just wasn't sure what to say to that. I don't want to fight with you anymore."

London sniffled. "I don't want to fight with you either. You're my best friend."

"You know how I feel about you, London. I only said those things because..."

"I know why you said those things and I know how you feel about Baxter," London interrupted. "But we shouldn't let that come between us. I'm still cookie."

Brenna chuckled. "It feels so good to laugh. These past few weeks have been so hard."

"I heard Seth moved out," London said.

"Yea. He came by today to pick up the kids to take to his mom's for the weekend. He told me you sold your Grammy's house. That's why I called. I was kind of shocked. How did you come to that decision?"

"It's a long story and I really need to get over to the house. I signed the papers today. Alma-Rae is being nice enough to give us the rest of the weekend to get everything moved out. I have so much packing to do," London said.

"We should do lunch tomorrow. If you have time."

"Or you can come over tonight and help me pack," London suggested. "Baxter is driving up to Ohio with Hadley and Denny. Denny's cousin owns a storage place. He's going to let us borrow one of his trucks and give us a deal on storage."

"Ohio? Why don't you just hire a local moving company?"

"I don't know. Baxter just wants to help Denny out. He's been out of work for a while and supposedly his cousin is going to pay him some kind of commission or something. I don't know. I think Baxter feels bad for him."

"He shouldn't," Brenna said.

"Well, I don't really mind if that's what he wants to do. That all might just be an excuse for some kind of bachelor party or something too. I don't know. It doesn't matter to me."

"You're suddenly very trusting."

"I'm trying to put those old habits behind me," London said. "Does that make me naïve?"

"No. I think it's a step in the right direction. I'm proud of you, London. I really am."

London was proud of herself too. All of her previous notions about love and marriage were gone. She was married to a wonderful man who loved her.

"Should I call tonight before I head over? Or just show up?"

"The phone is shut off over there already, so you should just come by whenever you're ready."

"I'll bring the pizza and wine. We'll have our own little bachelorette party too." Brenna laughed.

"I love it. Sounds great."

"Good. I will see you later, Cookie."

"Bye Brenna."

Pizza, wine, and a bachelorette celebration sounded better than an evening alone packing her memories into boxes. Baxter and the boys left town after work at around five-thirty. London spent the next three hours waiting for her friend to show up. Brenna had no way to reach her by phone to let her know she was running late, so London didn't immediately get upset when she didn't hear from her. When Brenna still hadn't arrived by ten o'clock, however, she got angry. She couldn't believe her friend would stand her up. She decided to confront her.

After a quick stop at the apartment to let Vienna go potty, London headed out to Whispering Trail. The lights at her dad's house were dark. Brenna's house was completely dark too. Was there a power outage? She didn't see any candles burning, but Brenna's car was in the driveway. London took a closer look as she started backing up. The front door was open. The door was only open a few inches, but that still seemed very strange. Something about this place gave her the creeps anyway.

London pulled her cell phone out of her purse to call Baxter; she was too scared to go into that dark trailer alone. No signal. Shit.

With her bright headlights shining toward the front of the mobile home, London inched her way slowly up the front steps. She called out to Brenna several times, but heard no answer. The clock on the VCR was flashing confirming there wasn't a power outage, but the front porch light wouldn't come on. The light bulb was missing completely from the end table lamp just inside the door. And the kitchen faucet was running. London was terrified, but concern for her friend compelled her further inside.

"Brenna. Are you okay?" she shouted.

London felt her way through the living room toward the kitchen. She turned off the water and felt around for the light switch. Fortunately, that light came on. The sink was empty except for a single jagged-edged knife. London immediately searched the counter and floor for blood. Thank God she found none.

"Brenna, if this is a practical joke it isn't..." London screamed out in terror as she stepped over the threshold into Brenna's master bedroom. Her friend... her best friend was slumped over the footboard on her bed with a telephone cord wrapped around her neck. She was dead. Strangled with a telephone cord just like in her nightmare. London had to reach Baxter. His life may be in danger too. A murderer was on the loose.

Chapter Sixteen

Adrenaline pushed London's foot down on the gas pedal and sent her speeding down that gravel road out of control. She couldn't believe Brenna was dead. She couldn't believe her best friend was murdered. London didn't want to imagine the last horrific moments of Brenna's life. She couldn't get that terrifying picture out of her mind. Who could have done such a thing? Seth? Brody? Denny? She tried urgently to reach Baxter on his cell phone, dialing and redialing his number until finally finding a signal strong enough for the call to go through.

"Please answer. Please Baxter. Please answer your phone," she pleaded. All she got was his voice mail.

That part of town was always quiet at this time of night. Few people lived in the area. A dense, natural orchard of sugarplum trees lined the highway on one side and on the other side a steep cliff overlooked the thriving Kenrickson Cove metropolis. London drove for miles without passing a single car, then finally she caught a break. She spotted the reflectors on the side of a police car parked at the end of a gravel road just inside the Coral Leaf city limits. She recognized the car immediately as Sheriff Dodd's and began flashing her lights and honking her horn. She slammed on her brakes and spun sideways toward the metal railing that guarded the edge of that steep cliff. Harrison jumped out of his car and ran to her.

"You could have killed yourself. What are you doing?"

"Brenna. Brenna," she replied breathlessly. She couldn't spit it out. She couldn't bear to say the words aloud. Brenna Reese was dead.

"Slow down, London. What are you doing out here in the middle of the night like this?"

London started again to try to answer, then realized she should be asking him the same question. There was nothing but deserted farm land at the end of that gravel road. Nobody had lived there in 20 years. Few people even travelled that stretch of highway; she had just witnessed that herself. What was he doing parked there in the darkness?

"I asked what you're doing all the way out here? Are you in some kind of trouble? Is it something with Brenna?"

"No. No. I just…" London got spooked. Harrison had a firm grip on her wrist with one hand. His other hand was unfastening the leather strap holding his pistol in place. Maybe he was the murderer. She pulled her hand away. "I have to go."

London jumped back into her car, shifted the car into first gear, and stomped on the gas pedal. The car jolted forward as she pulled her other foot off the clutch, but she managed to keep the car running. She barely got her car door closed before speeding away. Her little red Mazda Miata was too conspicuous. She knew it was only a matter of time before he found her. She tried again to reach Baxter, but still no luck. She hoped he wasn't already dead.

The Blankenship Car Wash was less than a quarter mile from London's apartment. The place closed at nine o'clock . The drive-through tunnel was the perfect hiding spot for her car. There were windows inside the lobby, but nobody could see in from the outside without actually driving through the parking lot. Harrison wouldn't think to look for her there. London pulled forward to the mid-point of the tunnel then jumped out and ran home to her apartment. Stress and horror sucked the air from her lungs as she bounded up the front apartment building steps. She couldn't catch her breath, but she couldn't let that stop her. She was running from a murderer.

Vienna didn't bark her usual greeting to welcome her home, but London was too disoriented at first to realize. She moved quickly through the darkness, waiting to turn on the lights until she was securely behind her bedroom door. That's where Geneva was waiting for her. Vienna was curled up comfortably in her lap; Geneva was feeding her bacon to keep her quiet. Baxter wasn't riding alongside a murderer. The sheriff of Coral Leaf was not a threat. The real danger was waiting for her within the walls of her own apartment.

"Why so scared, London?'

London cried out her fear and stumbled back against the wall. "What are you doing here? You scared me to death."

Geneva rose to her feet. She tossed a strip of bacon across the room and shooed Vienna into the corner. "That's an interesting choice of words."

"How did you get in here?"

"Oh, I've been planning this for a long time." Geneva laughed then started singing, her melody halting at times as though she was turning the handle on an old toy jack-in-the-box. "London bridges falling down. Falling down. Falling down."

"What the hell are you doing?"

"London bridges falling down…" Geneva kept singing and circling London as though she was on the brink of insanity. Then she stopped abruptly and with an evil smile on her face lunged backward and slammed into London with all her might. They both fell to the floor. London hit her head. Geneva laughed.

"What the…"

"Shut the fuck up," Geneva demanded. She wrapped her hands tightly around London's throat, pressing firmly against her windpipe. "You and me are gonna' take a little ride. See."

London squirmed trying to break free. Geneva just tightened her grip.

"This will go much easier if you relax, London. You saw what happened to your friend when she resisted," Geneva said. "The bitch got nosy and started poking around on the internet. She was going to ruin the whole thing,"

The room was spinning. London was starting to lose consciousness. She scratched at Geneva's hands trying to free herself. Geneva loosened the pressure against her windpipe. She relented a little at first then released her grip completely. London rolled onto her side, coughing and gasping for air.

"Now here's how it's going to go. You're going to walk out of here with me real cool like and get into Denny's old jeep. If you make any trouble, you are dead."

London kicked Geneva as hard as she could, but she didn't catch her off guard as she'd hoped.

"I said you're dead. Do you understand that, London? Dead!"

"What's the difference? You're gonna' kill me anyway."

"Well that all depends how useful you are." Geneva smirked and yanked London up off the floor by her hair. "Now get up. We have some place to be."

London went along with little resistance, hoping to buy time for Baxter to save her. She had no idea where they were going or how he was going to find her, but she held on to faith that her life was not going to end this way.

Denny Chapman lived in Conners Bluff on the other side of Lake Amethyst and not far from the Ohio River. That's where Geneva was taking them. He'd alienated his neighbors such that they all built a six foot privacy fence between their property and his. He wasn't likely to have visitors. They weren't likely to be disturbed. Geneva forced London into a kitchen chair then punched her three times hard in the face. London fought the urge to cry.

"You're never going to get away with this," London said. Blood dripped from her nose and bottom lip.

"You always underestimate me," Geneva replied, rubbing her knuckles dramatically. "Actually, everybody does. But it really pisses me off when you do it."

"Denny and the guys are on their way back from Ohio."

"Oh, London. You are so easy." Geneva sighed heavily and clapped her hands. She yanked the long phone cord from the kitchen wall and looped it around her arm.

London wasn't going to let things end this way. She wasn't going to give Geneva the satisfaction. But she wasn't fast enough. Geneva grabbed her as she sprang from the chair.

"Sit down, you fucking bitch!" She hooked the cord around London's neck and forced her back to a seated position, then used the excess cord to tie her hands to the back rungs of the chair.

"You are fucking crazy," London grunted.

"Yes, but I'm about to be fucking rich too," Geneva said, kicking London as she completed the final knot in her makeshift restraint.

Geneva strutted casually over toward the bedroom door. She was still singing that damn nursery rhyme and laughing. London had no idea what awaited behind that door. Something frightening. Something deadly. She squirmed in her chair, panic-stricken and trying desperately to free her hands. She knew she was about to die, but refused to beg for her life.

"What are you going to do when Denny gets back? He's even crazier than you are, Geneva. What are you going to do then?"

"I don't think we have to worry about that," she said.

Geneva grasped the handle and opened the door. There was Denny Chapman. He was dead too, shot in the head. London screamed and fought harder against the cords around her hands.

"Hadley isn't coming back either. Somebody cut the poor guy's brake line and oops... right off the side of the mountain." Geneva leaned back against the outer frame of the closet door and laughed hysterically.

"You are never going to get away with this," London repeated.

"I think we will get away with this. See, you came over here to confront Denny because he was threatening to go public with your fling," Geneva said. She grabbed a remote control from Denny's coffee table and sat down on the floor just beyond

London's reach. She turned on the television and pressed play on the VCR.

London immediately closed her eyes. She heard moaning and grunting. She didn't want to see what was on that tape.

"You're missing the best part, London."

London kept her eyes closed, but suddenly felt Geneva's breath on her neck.

"Open your eyes, London."

London refused.

"Open your fucking eyes, London!"

Geneva kicked her and knocked the chair over onto its side, twisting London's arm and pinning it broken beneath her body. She screamed out in pain and opened her eyes instinctively. There on the television she saw herself. In her room. On her bed. Denny was on top of her. She blinked the tears from her eyes. She had to be imagining things. What she was seeing was not possible.

"You two had quite a party," Geneva said. "Well, I guess Denny was the one having the party. You can't really tell by the video, but you were passed out there. You were just laying there like a dead fish. And I think Denny kind of preferred it that way."

"Turn it off," London demanded.

"You should have seen his face when I asked him to fuck you. I guess Baxter wasn't the only one with his eye on you."

London was crying. The pain in her arm was unbearable. The scene unfolding on screen was horrifying. "You are *never* going to get away with this. Baxter is going to fucking kill you."

"Gee, London. You jumped right to the really cool surprise," Geneva said excitedly. She got down on the floor, leaning in close to London's face. "He's kind of in on this... *with* me."

"You're a damn liar."

"No. Really." Geneva laughed. "Your marriage was all part of the plan. If you died and I inherited all the money, people would automatically suspect that I had something to do with it. I wouldn't be able to sell the house. But see now you and Baxter are married. You sold the house and now he and I get to split the money. So I get my half and I get your half."

London's head was spinning. This wasn't possibly true. Baxter couldn't fool her. She'd been trained by Brody – the master of deception and manipulation.

"Denny sent a text to his momma just an hour ago telling her that he'd done something really really bad and that he didn't think he deserved to live anymore," Geneva said. "They're going to find your bodies here and his finger prints all over the gun."

"You are out of your fucking mind."

"Aw, I made you upset. This will make you feel better. Baxter said you're the best fuck he's ever had." Geneva leaned over her and wrapped her hands around London's neck again. "Which is part of the reason I'm going to enjoy this so much. I had him first. He loved me first."

London closed her eyes and prayed. That' when she heard someone kick in the front door. Then a gunshot. She opened her eyes. "Baxter," she pleaded.

Geneva smiled broadly. "Hi, baby. I was just explaining..."

"Stop," he ordered, pointing the gun at her.

"What are you doing, baby? It's me. Your little honey bee."

Baxter pulled the trigger. London closed her eyes tightly, certain she was the target for the deadly bullet. Then a thump as Genova fell hard to the wooden floor without a scream or a murmur. London started screaming and crying uncontrollably.

Baxter untied London's hands and began slowly helping her up from the floor. "She's dead. She can't hurt you now," he said, guiding her to the couch as she cradled her fractured arm. He kissed her softly on the forehead

"You should have heard some of the crazy stories she was telling. She almost had me convinced that you were a killer. And that the two of you were in cahoots, planning to steal my inheritance. I'm so glad you found me."

London paused. There was an obvious question she was afraid to ask.

"How *did* you find me anyway? How did you know to look for me here at Denny's house?"

She could feel Baxter's body tensing. He didn't answer.

"Baxter, what's going on?" London tried to pull away, but he had her hair clinched in his hand and wouldn't let go. "What are you doing? Baxter?"

Baxter grumbled. "I never should have trusted that stupid bitch. She almost ruined everything so many times."

London fought him, but his strength overwhelmed her. He pointed the gun at her head and forced her to her feet. "Just shoot me. Get it over with."

"You were supposed to be dead already before I even got here, but I guess there's no harm in one more goodbye fuck."

Baxter lifted her effortlessly, tossed her over his shoulder, and carried her into the bedroom. She kicked and scratched. He threw her onto the bed and started tearing at her clothes, but she managed to break free. He caught her and slammed her head against the wall; the impact stunned her and knocked her down to her knees. London was crying and pleading with him to stop. He dragged her across the floor by her hair. Her eyelids were heavy. Light was fading in and out. She could feel blood streaming down her face.

"Please. I don't want to die," she whimpered. As she starting losing consciousness, London heard a second gunshot.

A familiar voice called out to him. "What's the matter, Baxter? You look like you saw a ghost."

The room went black.

Chapter Seventeen

London had no memory of anything that happened that night. She awoke many hours later in the hospital. A young brunette was sleeping in the arm chair beside her bed. She didn't recognize the woman. She didn't even have any idea why she was in the hospital. She reached out to the nurse who had just stepped into the room to check her IV.

"Who is that?" London whispered.

"I don't know, miss. I just came on duty thirty minutes ago."

The stranger opened her eyes. She smiled at London with an incredible look of relief. The girl's face looked familiar, but she had no idea who she was.

"Do I know you?" London asked.

"Not exactly," she said. She stood up and moved to the edge of the bed. "But I'm your sister. Geneva."

London stared blankly at the woman. Did she have brain damage or something? Had that whole ordeal been a long nightmare?

"I'm your *real* sister," she said. "That other woman was my roommate, Adrienne."

"I don't understand," London said. "Where is my husband?"

"Adrienne and her boyfriend tried to kill me. Then they came here and tried to kill you too. They wanted our grandmother's money."

London squinted her eyes. None of this made any sense. "Who are you? Really?"

"My name is Geneva Charles. My roommate was Adrienne Tripton. Her boyfriend was the man you married."

"Baxter? Baxter Bruce?"

"They are con artists. They were wanted in three states."

London reached out for the nurse's arm. She was confused and frightened. She had no idea who this woman was and what she wanted. "This has to be a mistake. Baxter and I are married and..."

"It's no mistake," the stranger said. "They're both dead."

London cried out. "Please get out. Get out. Please."

The nurse confronted the woman calmly and suggested that she leave. Alma-Rae entered the hospital room at that moment and stopped her. "She's telling the truth, sweetie."

"Where is Baxter? Where is he?"

"He's dead. They're both dead," Alma-Rae said.

London cried for reasons she couldn't quite understand. Nothing she was hearing made any sense. The person she thought was Geneva wasn't her real sister? The person who drove her crazy and pushed her to sell her family's property wasn't really her sister at all? The man she married wasn't who he said he was either?

"What about Brenna? Is Brenna..."

Alma-Rae walked around to the side of London's bed and grabbed her hand. "I'm so sorry, London. She didn't make it."

"Oh no."

"They haven't found Hadley's body yet, but they spotted his car..."

"Off the side of the cliff," London interrupted.

Alma-Rae nodded. "Yes. On North Route 13. Did Adrienne tell you that?"

London remembered that detail from her dream, but pretended otherwise.

"Where's Vienna? Is my dog okay?"

"She's fine, London. The sheriff found her at your apartment. She's at my house, safe and sound," Alma-Rae said.

The real Geneva spoke again. "I tried to save your friends. I followed you all for weeks. I just couldn't get to them in time and risk losing sight of you. I'm sorry."

"It was you? You were the one watching me?"

Geneva reached out and held London's hand.

London studied the girl's face. She saw pain. She saw remorse. She saw the family resemblance. "You look like my mom. And my Grammy."

"*Our* mom," Geneva corrected.

Both girls had tears in their eyes. Alma-Rae was beaming proudly. "There's somebody else here who wants to see you, London. I think you remember him. My brother Harlan."

Harlan Wickerford hadn't lived in West Virginia in more than 15 years. London knew him, but the feud between her grandparents and old man Wick kept her from knowing much about him. She was confused by his presence there at the hospital and even more confused about why he was holding her mother's painting.

"I wanted to give you this back," he said. "I know it meant a lot to your family. Alma-Rae found it left behind in my bedroom and…"

Alma-Rae tried to explain, but apparently found difficulty coming up with the right words. "I called Harlan when I found the painting because… well…"

London interjected. "You *are* my father."

Harlan nodded. "That painting is the view from my bedroom window. That's where she and I fell in love."

"Le Coeur du Lac," London whispered. Her eyes widened as she tried to swallow the big lump in her throat. She always sensed there was more to that painting than what Grammy told her. Harlan confirmed that as he described his feelings for Sicily

"Sicily was the one and only true love of my life," he said. "I knew that from the day I met her on the first grade playground. I wanted to marry her. Your grandfather said no."

"Why? Why would Grampy say no?"

"Because we were still in high school and I was going away to college in the fall."

"I didn't know any of that," Alma-Rae said. "I never even knew you had feelings for each other. I thought we were a threesome."

"So what happened?" London asked. "Mom was 28 when she had me."

"I was going through an ugly divorce," Harlan said. "I turned to your mom for comfort. She got pregnant. Vera and my dad were trying to protect me. And trying to protect the family money."

"So you just abandoned me?"

"I wanted to tell you after your mom died. Vera told me not to. She promised she'd take care of you and make sure you had a good life." Harlan sat down on the edge of the bed next to London. She gazed up at him, noting the expression on his face as he explained the deal he made with Grammy. She recognized that expression. She saw it often in the mirror. "I paid for everything. Your school. The house. My old man thought it was ridiculous."

"That's why he and Grammy didn't get along."

"That's right," he said.

Alma-Rae put her hand on her brother's shoulder. "When I saw the painting propped up against the window and I saw the view... well, I put two and two together."

"Is this for real?"

"I know that's a lot to throw at you in one day, London. But we felt like you needed to be surrounded by family. Real family," Alma-Rae said. "And I didn't want you to worry about your Grammy's house."

Harlan chimed in. "Since you are technically a Wickerford, your grandma's property and that house is still yours."

"The money is yours too," Alma-Rae said, putting her hand on Geneva's shoulder. "And you too, Geneva. You're going to get your fair share too."

London thanked Alma-Rae and Harlan, then reached for her sister and hugged her tightly in her arms. She felt at peace. Everything her grandmother had told her about the importance of family finally made sense. The girls had a long road ahead as they got to know each other and the town tried to recover from the lives lost so tragically. Still, London knew for sure that Grammy was smiling down proudly at that moment. London had her baby sister back. Grammy's little "Funshine Bear" had come home and there was light again in that place where darkness once cast a shadow.

Made in USA - Kendallville, IN
1076831_9781492110118
04.13.2020 0924